Jane Wondered When

Jane Wondered When

by

Laura Winters

Copyright 2025 by Laura Winters

All Rights Reserved
Including the right of reproduction in whole or in part in any form

This is a work of fiction. Some events have been compressed or altered. All the characters, names, and dialogue contained within this novel are the products of the author's imagination, or used fictitiously in this work, including any characters representing an agency, institution, or corporation. The opinions expressed by those characters should not be confused with the author's.

ISBN: 9798269242712
Edited by May Lan Tan
Book cover design and typesetting by Robert Allen @n23art
Cover art by Karen Hickey

To John

"Loud, loutish lover. Treat her kindly." Morrissey.

"With Annachie Gordon I'd beg for my bread
And before I'll marry Sultan, it's gold to my head
With gold to my head and gowns fringed to the knee
And I'll die if I don't get me love, Anachie."
Child 239, Round 102.

CHAPTER ONE
Late Bloomer

    Jane Mythen had begun to wonder if she'd ever meet a man who would seek out her company and pursue her relentlessly. Her two most recent relationships had been utterly underwhelming. Initially, the men in question had made their interest abundantly clear, but as soon as she'd started to like them back, they had become complacent and lazy. On paper, she would not budge when it came to fulfilling her standards; in reality, she was willing to give pretty much anyone a chance. While she'd found one of the two mildly attractive, the other man had held absolutely no appeal for her. She had been mistaken in presuming that an unattractive man would value her even more.

    Jane wasn't the first woman to think that a weak-chinned man with a dangerously low hairline would make for a more ardent admirer than a man who could match her in looks. Nor was she the first to discover that an insecure man will often seek external validation. And that to such a man, the attention of another woman will seem too rare and precious not to capitalise upon. These relationships had followed her divorce in quick succession and had been short-lived and unsatisfying. When, after a handful of dates, each man had withdrawn from her life without explanation or apology, only her pride had suffered.

    Daniel had been her first real boyfriend; she was a late bloomer.

During the second year of her Master's, Jane had fallen slowly and unexpectedly in love with him. The way his beady, deeply set eyes (which prevented him from being considered classically good looking) followed her as she entered the English literature wing of the library, and the intensity of his stare, had alerted her to the possibility that he might be holding a flame. She thought she had found the man of her dreams. She couldn't imagine life without him. He was incredibly sweet, and she couldn't imagine him even glancing at another woman.

At twenty-seven, being the first in her group of school friends to walk down the aisle had been gratifying for her and affirming for her mother. When they had been married for almost three years, Jane thought Daniel was going to ask her if she'd like to start a family. Daniel was a solicitor with a pretty respectable law firm in Dublin. Everything was going to plan. Instead, Daniel confessed that he was in love with Hilary Hopkins, a recently engaged associate solicitor at the same firm who was five years his junior.

His affair with H-squared, as Jane's friends now referred to her, had lasted for the duration of their marriage and may even have preceded the wedding. Hilary was the kind of girl that teenaged Jane would have considered pretty – the type of woman that men instantly liked. She was attractive in a very conventional way, even though she had the most regrettable dress sense. Her hair resembled an overblown mushroom; all puffed up at the crown and flicking outwards just above her shoulder. Seven years had passed since Daniel had told Jane his heart lay with someone else, fumbling his way through a half-hearted apology.

She had lost her trust in men, a little, but that was not the hardest part. The hardest part was that she had lost all faith in her ability to judge people and situations. How would she ever be able to rely on her instincts about choosing a man, when she had been so incredibly wrong about this one? She had always been so certain of his loyalty. His many female friends had not cost her a second thought in all the years they'd been together. She wondered if he had been casually unfaithful as well, or if H-squared had really been *the one*, as he had thoughtlessly described her on that fateful day. Jane wished she could retroactively find some evidence of his untrustworthiness – a sign she'd missed, perhaps. Armed with this knowledge, she'd surely find it easier to avoid making the same mistake.

Her mother, Claire, had said that some men simply were weak. Despite his good intentions and his desire to be loyal, Daniel lacked self-control. She had also conceded that Hilary was *alright looking*, which was Claire's way of saying someone was attractive. Her loyalty to Jane would not permit her to acknowledge the other woman's beauty outright. Jane had, of course, asked her mother's opinion, which was a habit she knew never served her well. The Christmas after the break-up, they had looked her up on Facebook over a glass of wine. Charlotte, Jane's sister, had described H-squared as pretty, which hurt Jane more than she ever could have imagined.

When Charlotte had suggested that Jane seek therapy, their mother had scoffed, declaring Jane not the type to share her feelings with a stranger. But Jane had welcomed the suggestion, feeling the need to reflect and make sense of the role she had played in this mess, even if this was just having unquestioning belief in her husband's infallibility. She was certain that a stranger, even an unqualified one, would help her more than her own family could. She resented her mother's insistence that she just move past it, and that the best revenge was to live a full and exciting life.

Jane eventually found a therapist to whom she could relate – a middle-aged woman called Jacq, whose warmth and humour made it a little easier for Jane to bare her soul. At first, they talked a lot about Daniel. Jane sometimes felt she was moving backwards and becoming angrier and more bitter as time progressed. She came to realise that therapy was an exorcism of sorts, akin to excising an ugly pimple. It had to get sore and inflamed before it could start to heal.

Just when she felt she'd turned a corner, she happened to see Daniel and Hilary leaving the cinema one evening. They were holding hands and laughing over some part of the film that they both found ridiculous. They looked happy, but no happier than she and Daniel had been in the first flushes of their love story.

To Jane's surprise, after about six months of abject misery, her heart had begun to open to the possibility of love. She no longer felt guilty about admiring a masculine man doing something manly. Daniel had always been a wimp, and that had bothered her. A drunken man had once made suggestive comments about her in a pub, tugging at the drawstring of her peplum top at the nape of her neck, sending shivers down her spine. Instead of defending her, Daniel had grabbed Jane's bag from beneath her barstool and bundled her out onto the street. She had felt a deep sense of shame at his cowardice. He would have been perfect if he weren't so lacking in masculine energy. These little memories eased the sorrow of being abandoned by someone she'd implicitly trusted.

After two years of weekly appointments, Jane plucked up the courage to tell Jacq that she felt ready to try living without the safety net of therapy. No matter how devastating her week had been, a chat with her therapist had never been more than six days away. Jacq had gently nudged her to return to her daily practices of drawing and reading. At first, she had placed her faith in traditional medicine alone, in the form of anti-depressants, but as she persisted in these pastimes, she found they were just as much a salve to her soul. A few months later, she picked up a pen and began to write again. That was when she truly felt herself.

It would be another two years before the divorce was finalised. When it came time to sell their apartment, Jane had expected Daniel to be amenable to her requests. After all, he had been the guilty party. She soon found that he had a spiteful side, which he'd hidden during their time together. When she asked him to give her six months to find a suitable place near her place of work and within her price range, he had snapped back that two was all she was getting. When her mother, Claire, phoned him to appeal to his better nature, he had roundly placed the blame for the demise of their relationship at Jane's feet. Upon hearing him label her daughter bossy and hostile, Claire, who rarely lost her composure, had called him a *bad bastard* before slamming down the phone. It was a phrase she had heard on a TV show. Claire's husband, Séamus, and both her daughters had never laughed so hard in their lives. Even Claire had tittered. To think of herself swearing in public, and in such an American turn of phrase.

Now, everything had been settled. With her parents' help, Jane had bought a delightful one-up, two-down in Greystones, a short drive from the school. It was pretty but in need of a lot of work. Although her mortgage was huge, she was confident that she would make the repayments every month. She had no intention of spending her salary on clothes and fancy restaurants, as Charlotte did. Jane would stay in on Saturday nights to watch classic films or read. Maybe she would finally write the novel she'd been promising herself she would, ever since Daniel left. She did not have much interest in marrying again. She had briefly tried the dating apps, and this pursuit had coughed up only two very forgettable men. She would bide her time and hold out for perfection. She had already accrued a lifetime's worth of disappointments. The next man would have to be magnificent.

She sported floral Victorian dresses and patterned stockings right through until the height of summer. Claire made no bones about her disapproval of her daughter's choice in clothing. Jane had inherited her mother's broad shoulders, narrow waist, and fulsome thighs. She had tried to offload some of her own, more fitted, suits on Jane when she was offered a permanent post in St Mary's.

Back when Jane was still only living with Daniel and they were engaged to be married, her mother had stood behind her at the long, oblong mirror in Jane's bedroom, gathering her dress so that it appeared more fitted around the waist. "Now, Jane, don't you think a girl like you who's slim around the middle should emphasise that?"

Jane had wriggled free of her mother's grip and ordered her to leave immediately. *I'm twenty-six and in permanent employment, for God's sake,* she thought. Of course, Claire hadn't been able to understand her daughter's reaction. It had only been a compliment, after all – a nudge in the right direction. The interaction had brought Jane right back to the age of twelve when, standing before the mirror, her mother had yanked hairpins from her hair and ruffled it as one might do to a dog or a child. "Much better. Your hair is your crowning glory," Claire had uttered in musical, drawn-out tones.

Jane had said nothing that day, but the message she received and buried deep inside was that since she didn't have a pretty face, it would be better to emphasise the one beautiful thing she had – her long, curly auburn locks.

Growing up, she had not been popular with boys or girls. She did have friends, but she was always a little different. Others sometimes mistook her shyness for snobbery. She wanted more than anything to fit in, but she found the conversations of girls her age dull and uninviting. She had a few friends in the year above, which only fuelled her classmates' suspicions that she thought herself superior to them. In truth, Jane thought she would be a lot happier if she were less intelligent. Surely, then, she would find much more enjoyment in the company of the dull-witted girls, who stood outside the one and only music shop in Glin on Saturday morning waiting for the local boys to finish rugby practice.

She was not most men's cup of tea. When she met Daniel towards the end of the second year of her Master's, she thought she had found her perfect match. Their mutual friend Sara had introduced them at the Student Union bar one quiet Tuesday afternoon. Daniel was two years Jane's junior, and an old school friend of Sara's younger brother, Thomas. The age gap was at first an issue for Jane but faded into insignificance as she listened to his anecdotes about his moody and delusional flatmate, who believed himself to be in a relationship with one of their law professors. Jane and Daniel exchanged pleasantries whenever they passed each other in the library or on the wider campus, but it was a full two months before she regarded him as a potential suitor.

The day he walked to her desk in the library and picked up a Milan Kundera collection of short stories she'd been reading, nodding his approval, she felt that destiny was finally manoeuvring in her favour. He admired a little sketch she'd done in the margin of her foolscap pad. She was flattered, particularly as she often doubted her artistic abilities. Her recognition of him as boyfriend material coincided fruitfully with the realisation that John Davy, her former love interest, was not waiting around for her. It seemed like divine timing, a message from above.

Daniel listened with a level of intent to which she was not accustomed, cocking his head to the side as he weighed her every word. He walked with a slight stoop, which endeared him to her even more, and he had a long, floppy fringe which made him appear sweet and non-threatening. He looked like the kind of young man who might be a classically trained pianist and a maths whiz. He hung out with Greg Behan, who was the Student Union president, and others of his ilk. They were loud and gregarious, which brought Daniel's charming humility into sharper relief. His movements were slow and measured. She couldn't imagine him ever losing his temper.

He was different from any of her other crushes. She could imagine him actually returning her interest. He seemed so manifestly happy to be in her company that she was certain he was bewitched by her. Her friends thought they were perfect together. He was somewhat taciturn, which added to his charm. Claire adored him, and even Charlotte had admitted that Jane had done well and chosen wisely.

When they got engaged, Jane felt a mixture of contentment and relief, if none of the excitement that most girls claimed to feel. Sara, their matchmaker, had reassured Jane that when something was right, it would feel comfortable and somewhat underwhelming rather than intense and exhilarating. Jane could see the sense in that. It felt fitting that by closing the chapter with John Davy, she had begun a new one with a different type of man.

As it turned out, Daniel could play only very rudimentary piano pieces and was not particularly gifted at maths. And, to her surprise, he did lose his temper quite often – always at home, and only ever with Jane. None of this really mattered, as by the time she realised these things, she had already fallen in love with him. She was mildly perturbed by the fact that on Saturdays, he never got up before two in the afternoon, and that he became irritated whenever she browsed for too long in a bookshop. He wasn't as well read as she had imagined. The last time he had read a full novel was when he had been at school. He preferred reading newspapers and history books to fiction. And yet, three years into their marriage she was just as certain that she had chosen the right man as she had been on their wedding day.

The most wonderful part of being married was that she would never have to go on a date again. Not that she had been on any real dates in college. Things were a lot less sophisticated back then. Most people met each other in grungy bars and, if they liked each other enough, met again the following week, and so on, until they were in an established relationship. For her generation, dates were definitely not a thing. Since meeting Daniel, she felt assured of her beauty, and cared little if men looked past her to her more conventionally pretty friends. She had Daniel at home. To him she was perfect, and that was such a blessing, she felt.

But her cavalier new attitude to her beauty and self-worth derived all its strength from Daniel's infatuation with her. She truly believed that in his eyes, she was the most beautiful woman to grace the earth. As soon as he told her that their marriage was over and that his heart belonged to someone else, all her childhood fears were immediately reinstated. She was a monster, gross and deformed, hence undeserving of love.

She knew she was of above-average height and that her hair fell somewhere on the colour spectrum between auburn and strawberry blonde. Beyond that, she had no idea if men considered her attractive. It certainly didn't seem so. She could count on the fingers of one hand the number of times she had been approached in a bar or a club. Her resting facial expression was one of composure, her mouth slow to form a smile. She was intelligent with a mind that easily alighted on a witty response, but her natural reserve and fear of causing offence caused her far too often to hold her tongue. Her gestures were graceful, her voice girlish with a barely perceptible lisp. Her skin was a milky white not usually remarked in red-haired people, and her eyes an alluring mixture of green and grey.

Despite having full lips, almond-shaped eyes, and a strong chin, Jane did not consider herself beautiful or even pretty. Certain discerning women in her life had presumed that carefully applied make-up would considerably enhance her already handsome features and had been disappointed to observe the opposite effect. Understatement was her thing – not only when it came to her appearance, but in every aspect of her life.

Jane had few friends, and that was by choice. While some women found her quiet self-assurance compelling; many perceived it as smugness. She preferred being alone with her thoughts and had no need for company a good deal of the time, which had the unintended effect of attracting hangers-on. Needy women often mistook her good manners for an invitation to approach. Before she knew it, she would find herself at a dinner party in the home of some woman she barely knew. She had considered that perhaps these newly acquired acquaintances recognised a want in her, but over the course of their one-sided friendship she would find greater evidence of their shameless desperation and eagerness to be heard.

On a dull October afternoon, Jane dolefully tipped the ash of her cigarette into the drain.

"Will I ever have a boyfriend, do you think, Mags? And be honest!"

Margaret Flannery was Jane's colleague and her closest friend. A history teacher who exuded warmth and kindness, her full cheeks and long, mousy brown hair, which she often wore in plaits, gave the impression of a much younger woman, a compliment paid her far too many times to have any effect.

"You've already had two boyfriends and a husband since I've known you. You make it sound like you've been single all your life," Margaret stated plainly.

"But they were awful! I didn't even like them," Jane reminded her before taking one long final drag of her cigarette and stubbing it out against the pebble dash of the gardener's shed.

Few people expected Jane, the very picture of health and moderation, to be a smoker. They felt that such unsavoury practices were better suited to a more laddish brand of woman who drank pints and indulged in the use of coarse language.

"You're so fastidious when it comes to getting rid of your cigarettes," Margaret observed wryly as her friend carefully pushed the butt through the grate. "It's a pity you aren't as careful when it comes to picking men."

Jane liked it when people teased her about her pernickety ways. "I don't want to give anyone grounds for complaint. Some people round here would love to catch me setting a bad example for the girls."

She was referring to Siobhán, the most senior teacher in Jane's department. Teaching was this woman's entire life; she appeared to have no other outlets. Jane genuinely liked her students and adored her subject, but she felt her heart was called elsewhere. She had never expressed her writerly ambitions to anyone else, not even to Margaret. She had scribbled a few unfinished short stories and had the outline of a novel hidden away in a Moleskine notebook in her writing desk at home. Only Siobhán sensed this. Always keen to weed out the true teachers from the aspiring novelists, she made sure to ask Jane on the first day of every new school year how the novel was going.

"Hmm, you're right, she would. Your department is so dysfunctional. You all hate each other, and Enid is your negligent mother, whose poor children are all vying for her attention."

Enid had been promoted to the position of department head, over the more senior and experienced Siobhán. Her style of teaching appealed primarily to the most talented of students who required neither notes nor guidance. For the rest of the students in her classes, she was an amenable yet disorganised mess, the butt of all department-related jokes and never around when needed. Siobhán, for all her pushiness, was reliable. Her notes were comprehensive, and she was always available from early morning till late in the evening, having no life outside of St Mary's. Jane fell somewhere in between the two extremes.

"You know, she's the type of woman who gives redheads a bad name. And I can say that as a fellow redhead. She's so vindictive."

During the most recent departmental meeting, Siobhán had seen fit to address Jane in front of everyone.

"Some of your students have come to me in confusion. They found a mistake in your notes on the play you are reading in class."

A typographical error was not the same as a mistake! Jane gritted her teeth as she relived the experience, wishing she'd called out Siobhán's attempt to humiliate her. Instead, she had feigned composure and politely thanked Siobhán for stepping in to save the day.

"Oh, you don't have to convince me," Margaret said. "I'm well aware of her limitations. Now, come on, let's get back before the bell."

The two young teachers walked with purposeful strides through the orchard and across the front lawn before slipping discreetly through a side entrance. They made their way to their respective classrooms where they taught the afternoon session. The view from Jane's classroom was exquisite. The vista of the ocean heartened Jane as she began the tortuous task of teaching Irish. This veritable thorn in her side was a requirement of her position. The terrified eyes of twenty nervous schoolgirls tracing her every movement, desperately hoping she'd forget to administer the grammar test with which they began each Friday's lesson. Jane was not a very good Irish teacher. A student had once complimented her on her teaching, likening her style to that of the Latin teacher. She'd smiled, the observation had been intended as a compliment, and so she had taken it in that spirit.

After all the worried First Years had shuffled out, the members of her senior English class nonchalantly filtered into the classroom. Some of the Sixth Years smiled sympathetically at the nervous juniors, with their heavy school bags almost as big as themselves. Some of them even brought large, bulky dictionaries to class, such was their eagerness to please their teacher. She pushed aside the colourful language textbook and pulled her copy of *Far from the Madding Crowd* from the shelf above her desk. Her heart lightened.

At times like this, she felt that life had been kind to her. Charlotte was a very well-paid accountant, who toiled away in a dreary office from nine till six each day. Here before her sat twenty eager young women, who hung on her every word, recording verbatim their teacher's casual observations about the text, as if her half-formed musings were literary gold.

Toward the end of the penultimate lesson of the day, Jane's phone beeped. She glanced at the screen. *Sender unknown*. She thought it was probably a reminder about her dental appointment on Monday. She slid the phone toward her, squinting slightly to decipher the small font. The text concluded with an exclamation mark and was signed off with an initial. It couldn't be an official message then, she thought. After a second or two, her eyes adapted to the text and she could tell with near certainty that this was how it read:

Hi Jane, long time no see! How's life with Glin's number one bookworm? J.

She knew immediately that the message was from a man. Jane didn't collect friends as some women do. She didn't hand out her number to people she'd met only once at teacher in-service days or in evening classes. She wouldn't have been against it, but people rarely asked. She gave the impression of someone who placed a premium on her time. Unbeknownst to her, it was the general expectation that Jane would have far too much going on in her life to make room for someone new. In reality, Jane was quite lonely at times and spent a lot of her time reading.

Only someone who expected you to have their number saved would sign off with an initial. Or perhaps it was an attempt to create intrigue. Whoever they were, they had certainly piqued her interest. She tucked the phone under her teaching diary and switched back into teacher mode. When the girl who had been reading came to a natural pause at the end of the paragraph, Jane craned her neck to one side and waited until she had the attention of the entire class.

"I want you to make three lists: one for Gabriel Oak, another for Farmer Boldwood, and the third for Sergeant Troy. You will list as many of their respective attributes as possible, backed up with solid examples from the text, and then you will choose our heroine's most suitable match."

"But we haven't finished yet! We don't know how they'll turn out," Julia, the anxious twin, voiced her concerns to a chorus of groans. Julia's far more easy-going twin, Grace, who slouched at the desk directly behind her, rolled her eyes dramatically.

"Well, we don't always wait until the end of life to make decisions. We make plenty of calls along the way. You can revise your choice later when you know more."

Jane suspected that Julia may have been the one who alerted Siobhán to the error in her study hall notes the previous week. She thought of how she had chosen to forget John Davy and make her life with Daniel. How certain she had been at the time that her choice was a well-informed and sensible one.

CHAPTER TWO
Memory Lane

As her mind explored the possibilities of this most recent contact, a soft, involuntary sigh escaped Jane's lips. The two prefects seated just in front of her desk glanced up at her. She quickly regained her equanimity and continued to silently read the passage in the book perched atop her knee. She had no time for misery when it came to literature; there was enough of it in the world as it was. She was seated on her desk with her feet resting on an unoccupied chair. She preferred to be near or amongst the students to remove the necessity of raising her voice. These small choices lent an air of accessibility to her teaching style.

As soon as the bell had rung and the students had exited the classroom, she would reread the message. To nurture any hope that the sender of this message was a man – possibly the one man whose memory she'd never been able to shake, and that he might still be eligible, would be not only foolish but downright reckless. And yet, the sky outside her window appeared brighter when she contemplated this remote possibility.

Jane greatly preferred *Middlemarch* to this novel at hand, always having felt that a male writer could never fully capture the complexities of a woman's character. But, in a departure from her usual method, she had allowed her students to choose the novel they would study this year, and the majority had chosen the shorter book.

They had met as teenagers, arriving for orientation at University College Dublin. He was reading law and she the Arts: English and History. Their eyes met across the student café. He had all the easy charm and confidence of a privately educated schoolboy, striding over to greet her. He knew her to see, he said. She had smiled meekly, registering mild disappointment that he couldn't recall her name.

She had not been part of the popular set back home. Her younger sister, Charlotte, would have comfortably chatted away to him, and Jane imagined he would have enjoyed her inane small talk. But, on a deeper level, she hoped that John was not looking for a girl like Charlotte – that he might want someone unique. By the time their brief and somewhat awkward conversation concluded, Jane had convinced herself that she would be that someone.

Over the course of the next three years, they remained amiable acquaintances. While he flitted from one obvious beauty to the next, she sat at home, waiting for him to realise that he and Jane would make the perfect couple. They lived on adjacent streets for a while: she in digs; he in a top-floor flat with two old schoolfriends.

One hazy June evening at the end of their second year, she had come close to kissing him at a party. The following week, he had left for Rhode Island to take up a summer job as a sailing instructor. Soon after, she returned to Glin. She spent three long and tedious months waiting tables in her father's pub, still hopeful that John would find his way back to her before the summer's end. By the time the leaves took on their golden hue and the air became crisp and dry again, this dream had evaporated.

The possibility that this message was from John Davy had sent her pulse racing. She resisted allowing such hope to enter her heart for even a moment. At times, she felt positive – anticipatory, even – about the prospect of finding love. But when it came to John, she couldn't bear to set herself up for the inevitable disappointment. John liked to be liked. He was ridiculously popular. She would have to distinguish herself from all the other women who were lining up for his attention. They all were bright, successful, and amiable. She had cultivated an air of intellectual superiority in his presence, the memory of which now burst her reverie and made her toes curl.

She had returned to that moment millions of times. On a Sunday night, just after the end of their summer exams, John's friend Roger had invited her friend Sara to an impromptu house party. As the girls got ready in Sara's bedroom, Jane was excited to let her inhibitions drop. She was wearing a new red blouse that complemented her luminous complexion and was feeling uncharacteristically confident and free.

"Are all his friends going to be there?" Jane enquired nonchalantly.

"Yeah, of course. It's a party, Jane," Sara said, outlining her lips with a pink pencil.

John was particularly drunk that night, standing with his back to the sash window as the girls entered the sitting room. John seemed surprised to witness this new version of Jane, her usual reserve shaken off with the aid of the half-bottle of white wine she had downed in Sara's kitchenette.

Roger brought Sara to an olive-green sofa and asked a large, solitary figure drinking a can of cider to make room for his friend, which the man did, begrudgingly. As Roger went off to procure a drink for Sara, Jane perched awkwardly on the arm of the sofa, hoping Roger would also bring her one, not least so that she would have something to do with her hands. To her surprise, he did. She had never liked Roger before this moment.

The sitting room was densely packed with young, attractive college students exhibiting varying stages of drunkenness. An extremely thin blonde girl, who was standing close enough to John that she could have examined his nasal cavity, looked boldly in their direction, her face a perfect picture of disgust. John was staring – surely at Sara or some other dainty blonde, Jane thought. She stole another glance in his general direction. There was no doubt but that he was staring at Jane. She felt a warm flush in her cheeks. The blonde girl gesticulated wildly, in time with a Jamiroquai song playing from a stereo in the corner. Jane, who found small talk particularly troublesome, felt a mixture of envy and awe in the presence of those to whom it came naturally.

"Look, Sara, is she dancing or talking?" Jane remarked wryly as she nodded in the girl's direction.

Sara snorted the type of instantaneous laugh that cannot be faked. It was a sound that Jane found very gratifying. "Well, if she's dancing, she needs to work on her moves." Sara's eyes flitted around the room, gauging the competition.

The girl turned again in their direction. Her lips visibly curled into a sneer.

"Oh, look at her now," Sara observed wryly. "She has it in for us! She must think we're here to take John from her."

"She's John's girlfriend?" Jane asked in disbelief. She found it difficult to fathom that John would go out with anyone who was insecure enough to be intimidated by her.

"Of course! In her head, though!" Sara stood up to greet Roger's sister and as the two girls walked off toward the kitchen, Jane hopped down off the arm of the sofa and into the empty space left by her friend. Sara weighed only about seven stone, so it was a tight squeeze, and Jane immediately regretted her decision. She caught a glimpse of herself reflected in the glass door of the liquor cabinet. She was heartened that the rosiness of her cheeks had not spread to her chin or neck, as sometimes happened when she felt flustered. And then, before she realised what was happening, she felt a weight on the arm of the chair. She looked up just as John Davy, who looked inebriated but undeniably handsome, leaned down to plant a clumsy yet endearing kiss on her cheek.

For all the time she had spent that summer dreaming about their reunion, she never truly believed, in her heart of hearts, that it would ever come to be. They inhabited two different worlds, which somehow collided on that balmy June evening. Now, sitting in her classroom all these years later, she wondered whether he remembered the frisson that had passed between them. Or, at least, how lovely she had looked in her red blouse. He seemed to have been captivated by her beauty that night, but he was also very drunk.

She had expected to encounter a little awkwardness the next time she saw him – some self-consciousness on his part, an implicit acknowledgement that something had changed between them. When they passed each other in the library tunnel a few weeks into the new term, she was met with his usual bright, casual indifference. His broad smile and cheerful nod took her aback. She attempted to match his breeziness but, for the first time in her life, was incapable of putting on a front. They looked at each other for what must have been a full ten seconds. The silence was excruciating. He seemed to be struggling to make sense of her reaction. She felt her cheeks flush.

He eventually found his voice. "How was your summer?"

"Oh, fine, thanks. You know yourself. Hard being back."

He grinned, apparently relieved now that the conversation

was back on an even keel. "Were you away?" His tone was friendly and detached. It was exactly what you'd expect from someone who didn't give a damn about you. He had not once thought of her over the summer, she now realised. How could she have gotten it so wrong? She was a fool to think he had any interest in her beyond a quick, drunken fumble.

"No." She was eager to cut short the charade. "I was working for my dad all summer."

"Ah, I love your dad's place!"

She knew he didn't. The summer after the Leaving Cert, he had come in for a drink with a few of his rugby teammates. They'd stayed for one round, or maybe two, before moving on somewhere more to their liking. She had been waiting tables that night, so he'd had ample opportunity to approach, but he'd acknowledged her only when it would have required more effort not to.

At that moment, a boy – it would have been disingenuous to call him a man – who happened to be gliding past them slapped John on the back before turning to point at him, all without breaking stride. John returned the gesture with a notable lack of self-consciousness. Jane would have been less embarrassed if they'd high-fived each other. She hoped that none of her classmates would pass by. She found their interaction offensive and, frankly, gross. It was clear that boys like John Davy and his pointing friend, in their Ralph Lauren shirts and twee, oxblood penny loafers, felt that the campus belonged to them. All the insignificant people, like Jane and her unobtrusive friends, were simply extras, filling in the space around them.

"Cooney! How the hell are you?" John hollered after his friend's retreating form.

He was grinning widely, showing his perfect white teeth. Jane couldn't bear the sight. In a rare moment of self-preservation, she touched him on the elbow, wished him well, and moved right on with her life.

Once or twice in the intervening years she had seen him, usually around Christmas time, and invariably with a new, maddeningly beautiful girlfriend. He had moved to London, then New York, for study and for work. She had gotten on with her life, to some degree, without ever fully relinquishing the dream that John would one day recognise the depth of his feelings for her. And yet, on some level not too far below the surface, she understood that they were not ideally suited for one another. John Davy was pompous and spoilt. Despite being bright, he lacked depth and creativity.

Upon meeting Daniel, she had laid to rest the ghost of John Davy – or so she had thought. She had been infatuated with John Davy only because he possessed everything she lacked: confidence, self-assurance, and popularity. With Daniel, it was a meeting of the minds. If anything, they were too much alike. They were both introverts who took a while to warm up in conversation with strangers. Neither of them held mass appeal to the respective opposite sex, but the admirers they had were ardent and certain.

When she sat beside Daniel, who remained completely absorbed in his history book, she felt a quiet sense of contentment unlike anything she had experienced. She felt secure in the knowledge that he would never leave her. Out of all the men she regarded as potential suitors, he was the closest to perfection, in her eyes.

The bell rang, and as the students started to filter out, Jane remembered she had a resource session with a junior girl who was struggling to fit in. The student had not received any specific diagnosis that would necessitate having a one-on-one class each week with Jane, but St Mary's was the type of private school where a student's emotional needs were taken almost as seriously as her academic ones. The student in question was the niece of the Chairperson of the Board of Governors. Unlike her uncle, she was reticent and shy, and tended to apologise profusely for taking up Jane's time.

On this Friday afternoon, she failed to appear. They had an informal arrangement, whereby Jane made herself available to chat at this particular time if the girl in question felt the need, and usually she did. After five minutes had elapsed with neither sight nor sound of the Chairperson's niece, Jane reached for her phone.

As she was rereading the message, her phone pinged. Another message appeared from the same number.

By the way, it's John Davy. From Glin. In case you're struggling to think of all the Js you've ever met!

Jane's heart made a leap of joy.

CHAPTER THREE
Girls' Talk

"So, what the hell is going on, Jane? I mean, a guy you haven't spoken to in fifteen years just texts you out of the blue?"

Margaret flicked the ash of her cigarette out the window before releasing the handbrake of her boyfriend's clapped-out Volkswagen Golf and manoeuvring it cautiously through the school carpark. Margaret had not driven her own car ever since it conked out in the car park of the shopping centre. As Frank cycled everywhere and found parking incredibly stressful, he had happily handed over the keys.

"I have no idea!" Jane examined her teeth in the small mirror on the interior of the sunshield. "Is it too good to be true?"

"How did he even get your number? Were you two ever actual friends?" Margaret frantically rubbed the windscreen with the back of one hand as she steered with the other.

"No! I mean, we knew each other to chat to, but no, not friends. But there was one time we came close to—"

"Sleeping together?" Margaret's voice jumped up an octave, betraying her utter shock.

The car jolted, prompting the two young women to laugh. Margaret was an erratic and emotionally charged driver, and Jane was getting a lift with her only because her own car was with the mechanic having a tune-up in preparation for the NCT.

"No, not at all." Jane felt quite embarrassed at having to admit this.

"Kissing, then?"

"No, not that either. I just had a feeling that he liked me. I mean, he gave me no reason to believe that he had any interest. I probably misinterpreted—" Jane's voice trailed off, and she sighed. The fact that they had merely exchanged a knowing look one night, when they both were fairly drunk, brought home the insubstantiality of the situation. How could she justify holding a permanent place in her heart for a man that she had never even kissed?

"Well, maybe so." Margaret shook her head slowly in disbelief, her eyes wide with wonder. "But he clearly likes you now, or he has realised that he liked you all along. I mean, why else would he be getting in touch?"

"Well, I suppose I did send him a friend request on Facebook. A bit desperate?"

"No!" Margaret slowed down to let another teacher cut in front of her before starting the journey down the long, tree-lined drive. "Sure, I'm friends with yer man in front on Facebook," she muttered, gesturing at the beat-up Peugeot ahead, "and I'm pretty sure I sent the request."

Jane knew that Margaret meant no disrespect to Donald Nephin, the middle-aged maths teacher, driving at a painfully slow pace down the school drive. He stopped to salute students, rolling down his window to have a word with one he hadn't seen in a while.

"Well!" Jane rolled her eyes dramatically. "Wait till you get a text from Nephin in the middle of your Sixth Year History class in a few weeks' time. Your boyfriend might not be too happy."

Margaret snorted with laughter. Jane could always count on her for reassurance and support. It was the thing she admired most in her friend, and an attribute she tried to cultivate in herself.

"You know, he would never have contacted me had I not reached out to him," Jane pondered aloud. "I sent him a request, and then I cancelled it a few days later, as he'd ignored it."

"Well, he must have gone to great lengths to get your phone number."

"It wouldn't have been that difficult. I mean, his sister and I have friends in common, and I used to tutor his younger brother in college."

"Still, when was the last time you asked a friend or a family member for someone's number? It definitely requires some effort. You two didn't have mobile phones in college, did you?"

"I didn't. I don't know if he did, but I always thought it a bit naff, walking around with a phone to your ear. I still do!"

"Hmm, yeah. I didn't get one till I started teaching here." Margaret waved at Donald Nephin as she turned onto the main road, leaving him waiting patiently to make his left turn.

"You love him," Jane teased Margaret. How she envied her friend's ability to befriend men of all ages.

Margaret turned to face Jane full on, something she habitually did while driving, which Jane found deeply unsettling. "Do you still have that gorgeous profile photo?" Margaret demanded.

"You mean the one where I don't look like myself?" Jane smiled wryly, aware that it was a very flattering photo. "Yes, I do."

"Oh, shut up! I'm feeling really positive about this, Jane. I'm thinking you guys are going to get married."

Jane guffawed. "Married? Are you joking? I'd be happy with a boyfriend, Mags. I don't think I ever want to be married again. It's completely overrated."

"It's Daniel that was overrated."

Just thinking of their life together, in the small Northside apartment they'd bought from his uncle, was enough to make her feel depressed. She couldn't quite understand why a memory such as this would cause her such acute pain. She was glad to be rid of Daniel. The image of him and H-squared looking into each other's eyes and holding hands, as they strolled down Parnell Street, was seared into her memory. They had both looked so cosy and content. All these years later, they were still together.

Jane had met Hilary only once before, at Daniel's Christmas party. She had worn large round glasses and an air of unnerving silence, and Jane had taken an instant dislike to her. The following day, Jane had texted Margaret to say she'd met a really creepy girl at the drinks party. While she had made no effort to talk to Jane, her eyes, wide and watchful, betrayed a hatred whose source had baffled Jane at the time.

"Yes, Daniel was overrated. I overrated him. But I still don't see the point of marriage."

Margaret was frantically twisting the knob for the aircon back and forth. Jane noticed that her friend's nail polish was chipped and unevenly applied. Margaret lived in Enniskerry, a small village not too far from St Mary's, with her boyfriend, Frank, who was fastidious and intolerant of mess. Margaret had told Jane of his little rants about the state of the bathroom sink or the presence of half-filled bottles of sparkling water scattered throughout their newly acquired three-bed semi. However did they get along? She imagined Frank returning from a work trip abroad to find his car in such disarray. Student copies were strewn across the back seat, and a hairbrush lay atop a crumpled crisp packet on the floor.

"He'll kill you, you know," Jane said, pointing out the crisp bag.

"I've told you; he has OCD. It's good for him to sit in a little bit of mess. It's like exposure therapy."

"Sure." Jane smiled. In theory, she certainly agreed with Margaret's take on the situation. Still, she would not have liked to witness one of his meltdowns. "I wonder if John asked Clodagh for my number?"

"That's his sister, right? And Rory's their brother?" Margaret had a forensic memory, especially for names. She liked to imagine how the different personages in her friends' lives looked and dressed. "You gave him grinds, right, for his Leaving Cert?"

"Yes, that's him. He had dyslexia, and a problem with his vision, so he fell behind in school. But he was actually quite clever."

"Why don't you date *him*, Jane? He sounds great."

Jane laughed half-heartedly. Margaret, for all her kindness and warmth, sometimes offended Jane's sensibilities with her casual cruelty. Jane had known Rory since he was a little boy. Her heart would melt at the sight of him, with his horn-rimmed glasses and one eye permanently patched, playing alone in the schoolyard. John had seemed never to notice that his brother wandered about by himself so much of the time. Or perhaps he had noticed but hadn't cared. This was something she disliked very much about John. It would have been so easy for him, to whom friendship came so easily, to help Rory out. The other children would have been impressed if they'd known that Rory was John's brother.

"Well, I have a gut feeling that this will all end in a church," Margaret said. "Just resist the urge to turn up for the first date in a wedding dress, OK?"

Jane let out a loud sigh. "I'll arrive naked."

They laughed. The air conditioning appeared to have stopped working altogether and Margaret had given up on twiddling the knob. As they sat in companionable silence for the remainder of the journey home, Jane wondered whether Margaret's light-hearted enthusiasm on the topic of marriage was an attempt to hide her own embarrassment.

Might she feel awkward that Frank had never thought to propose? It was possible. Then again, Margaret was not a traditional person; she was highly practical. She had been keener to get on the property ladder than to walk down a church aisle in a ridiculous white dress.

At a bridge night a decade and a half earlier, Claire Mythen, often described as a force of nature, was making her way to the scoreboard to see how she and her partner had fared in the weekly competition run by the club. While not a particularly artful player, she was a competitive one, nonetheless. Paula Davy stepped into her path abruptly. Both women had shoulders as broad as their husbands' and were blessed with pretty features sometimes overlooked in their plump faces. In fact, people often mistook them for one another. Each woman mistakenly presumed the other to be terribly flattered by the comparison.

As Claire, being too preoccupied with her own thoughts to take offence, began to walk around the woman whose identity she had barely registered, Paula took hold of her elbow, and a very brief conversation ensued. Its outcome was an agreement that Claire's eldest daughter, Jane, would tutor Paula's youngest son, Rory, in English and Irish each Friday for the remainder of the final school term.

While the other Davy siblings were flying high, poor Rory had struggled through school. He had set his heart on a career as a primary teacher and Paula felt that the work and the lifestyle would suit him better than a nine-to-five job; however, Rory's tutor had advised against him sitting the Higher-Level Papers. After a fraught exchange, Paula had dispensed with his services, and now she needed to find someone fast. Paula had always liked Claire's eldest daughter.

Jane's small group of friends were now too busy with their new internships or boyfriends, or both, to make time for her. Two new girls had moved into the digs with her. They had been best friends since childhood and had brought along a television, which they installed in the large front bedroom that they shared. They loved Australian daytime soap operas and studied every night between seven and ten. They never socialised.

Jane spent every weekend holed up in her room, pretending to be studying or writing. The landlady, a middle-aged civil servant from Cavan, who was perpetually on sick leave from her post in the Department of Agriculture, encouraged Jane to get out more. Jane was too embarrassed to tell the woman that she simply did not have any friends left in Dublin. When Claire rang the landline one Friday evening to see if her daughter would be interested in tutoring Rory Davy, Jane jumped at the chance. She was quite relieved to have a reason to come back to Glin.

Margaret cut across two lanes of traffic to take the turn for Mill Lane. Two drivers honked their horns in annoyance.

"Fuck off," she mouthed aggressively in the rearview mirror.

"Jesus, Margaret. You need to chill out." Jane was a nervous passenger and her friend's casual disdain for the rules of the road unnerved her. "Anyway, I'm sure it was Clodagh who passed on my number. She has always been so grateful to me for helping Rory."

Margaret pulled up to the kerb. "So, does he teach in a regular primary school now? With kids?"

"No, actually, Mags. Retired sailors and the unwaged!"

"You know what I mean, though. Some of those small private schools, they'll employ anyone. Like yer one, Nicola. She qualified in the UK, and she has no Irish, but sure they don't care about that, once you have the right accent."

Jane sighed as she brought their former colleague to mind. Nicola Plummer had taught religion with them in St Mary's for a while. Her plan had been to get a post in one of the feeder schools in the area. Last they heard, she was vice principal of one such little Protestant school. As word had it, she was already engaged to the local vicar's son.

"I wouldn't put him in the same class as Nicola. I mean, he's a nice guy. She's basically a psychopath." Jane nervously looked over her shoulder to see if her neighbour had come to his window. He was fanatical about parking, and no matter how many times Jane asked Margaret not to park directly outside his house, she persisted in doing so.

"Why now?" Margaret exclaimed in a dramatic TV journalist voice as Jane hurriedly gathered up her belongings. "What's piqued John Davy's interest after all these years? Have you been posting topless selfies on Facebook again, Jane Mythen?"

"I can assure you I have." Jane smiled, looping the handles of her canvas bag over her shoulder as she gently closed the passenger door.

Margaret laughed heartily, pulling out without as much as a glance over her shoulder.

Jane entered her pretty cottage. It had originally been built in the 1920s for local rail workers, and she never tired of its pretty sash windows and exposed beams. Her father had painted it, and her mother had made the loveliest curtains for the sitting room windows. Jane's parents were not demonstrative people, but when Daniel left her, they did everything they could to make her life as easy as possible.

She had been a sensitive child and had always felt a disconnect with them. They didn't understand her or her concerns. Her sister, Charlotte, was easier, more straightforward, if a little spoilt and demanding. Jane became so upset at the smallest of things, the minutest alteration to plans. But her father, Séamus, a plainspoken man who was shy but well-liked, could see himself in his taciturn daughter who struggled to make friends and preferred her own company.

Jane threw her bag of copies on the sofa and regretted not having tidied up after herself that morning. She loathed cleaning, but could not live in anything but a spotless, dustless environment. Were it not for her hefty mortgage repayments, she'd hire a cleaner. If she ever wrote a novel and became rich and famous, she'd have a full-time housekeeper. Life was too short to spend it dragging a vacuum cleaner up and down that steep staircase. She set herself the task of quickly completing twenty small jobs, which included emptying the dishwasher, loading it with dirty dishes from the sink, sweeping breadcrumbs from the countertop onto the floor, and finally hoovering the entire downstairs.

Growing up, Jane had never been popular with boys. She was tall, awkward, and standoffish. In a world where being different was social suicide, aloofness was her only form of self-defence. Glin had two primary schools: the Catholic one, where all the ordinary folk, including Jane and her sister, went; and the Protestant one, where the teachers did a lot of arts and crafts, and cared deeply about the child's experience of learning.

John had initially attended the Protestant one and then had joined St Fiachra's in fourth class. His parents had grown disillusioned with the creative education he was receiving and wanted him to be more thoroughly prepared for secondary school. He would attend Glenstal Abbey, as had his father, four uncles, and his older brother, before him. An entrance exam would determine in which stream he'd be placed.

Everyone knew that John was bright. His father was the local doctor, and his mother had been a geography teacher in Ballybunion, a small seaside town across the county border in Kerry. "The teachers can only bring you as far as they have come themselves, and not beyond," his mother had said at the time. Jane's mother had thought it snooty to presume a ten-year-old boy was brighter than his teachers.

Much to the shock of Jane, who prided herself on being the top achiever in her class, John soon outshone her in everything except English and Irish. He had an agile mind that seemed most at ease with numbers. Jane's brain resisted numerical problems, preferring instead to deal with words, where there was room for more than just one right answer. How unfair that someone could be that popular, rich, and brilliant! Not to mention the fact that he was also good-looking.

Jane and John were placed side by side at the same desk, where they were allowed to work ahead in the textbook. John was pleasant and gracious in a way that only an adored, youngest son could be. Except that John wasn't the youngest son; there was another four years his junior, whom their mother rarely mentioned. Word was he had special needs, but, as Jane quickly came to realise when she tutored him many years later, he was simply average.

How hard must it have been to be the average one in a family of geniuses. Rory was unathletic and skinny, with red hair and freckles. In fact, he had a very nice face, as Jane came to recognise later. Sometimes she thought Rory was more traditionally handsome than John, but her heart was firmly with the older brother by that stage.

For secondary school, she was sent to the local girls' convent, and John went to a posh boarding school. After that, they saw very little of each other. When their paths occasionally crossed at a tennis club disco or the local hotel swimming pool, he saluted her and smiled generously but never used her name. Perhaps he couldn't remember it. They had been in class together for only three years. Girls invariably gathered around, unashamedly waiting their turn to exchange pleasantries and flirt with John, who was not at all embarrassed by the attention.

A red light was flashing on the landline phone, which meant her mother had called and left a voicemail. She would expect a return call before the soaps started at seven-thirty. Her mother talked and talked, without really saying much. There was always a gossipy air to her chatter. Claire Mythen did not celebrate the good fortune of others, and she was loath to pay anyone a compliment, behind their back or to their face. Although her stories could be entertaining at times, they were never uplifting.

When she had been eleven or twelve years of age, Jane had gotten caught up in a crowd of locals as they filtered out of the town hall at Hallowe'en. She couldn't remember the exact occasion, but she had a feeling it was a fundraiser of some kind. Her mother's name was mentioned. Jane turned just in time to catch the listener in this tête-à-tête throw her eyes to the heavens, and whisper, *What an absolute bore!*

This encounter had left a lasting impression on young Jane. From that moment on, she couldn't help but notice how insufferable her mother could be. Jane squirmed whenever Claire would mention, as she frequently did, her tenuous relationship with a local bishop. He was a very distant cousin of her mother's, and had, at Claire's request, said mass in their home once before Christmas when Jane was six or seven. She hadn't made her First Holy Communion yet. She recalled him laying his hand on the crown of her head for what seemed like an eternity, wishing her a very happy day and telling her he'd remember her in his prayers, which she very much doubted. When the scandal broke about his love child, Claire Mythen erased all traces of him from her life. It was as if he had never existed, which was a great relief to Jane, as none of her friends' mothers were particularly impressed with her ecclesiastical namedropping.

After watching an hour or two of unsatisfactory home renovation television, Jane texted her mother to apologise for not having returned her call, promising that they would talk the following day, and wishing her well in her bridge competition. Then, she slipped beneath the floral quilt Claire had bought her the previous Christmas. Although she would never spend such an exorbitant amount on bed linen, she appreciated her mother's expensive tastes.

She allowed her mind to wander back over the events of the day. There was only one of real significance: John Davy's message. Would he be offended by her lack of response? She had no idea how to play this, whatever *this* was. She had a strong suspicion that it was a game. She should wait until tomorrow to respond. He had kept her waiting for almost two decades, after all. Should she be herself? Was she too old to play hard to get? These questions ricocheted in her mind until she finally surrendered to sleep.

"Good morning, Jane!" Claire's sweet tone belied her often caustic tongue. "Did you have a good night's sleep?"

"Oh, not bad," she lied, for a reason unbeknownst to herself.

Was it possible that she enjoyed the attention her mother had started to pay her in recent years? Claire had switched her focus from her own health to that of Jane's. Jane's childhood had been punctuated by her mother's health scares. These were only ever scares. First, cancer; then, arthritis; then, one undiagnosed virus after another. There were months of anxiety, followed by short bouts of intense relief that Claire wasn't seriously ill after all, and then, the arrival of new and different symptoms, which threw life back into disarray.

"You really should take magnesium, Jane. It relaxes your body and—"

"Yes. I might pick some up later." Jane looked around her bedroom for inspiration, hoping to transition to a non-health related topic.

Before she could think of one, her mother had already started down her usual path. "Well, I was listening to the radio this morning. And they had a health expert on, a gut specialist..."

Jane, who was no longer listening, tuned out her mother's voice and simply uttered an *um* or a *really* whenever her mother paused for breath. Finally, she plucked up the courage to take the reins.

"I have buckets of corrections," Jane interjected, realizing a moment too late that buckets were used to convey an abundance of something positive, such as charm, or cash. She felt safe in the knowledge that her mother would not notice such a subtle error.

"Oh, for God's sake, Jane. You shouldn't be bringing work home with you at the weekend. I mean, other professions don't do it." Her mother had an opinion on everything and everyone.

"Oh, it's a busy time in school, Mum." Jane thought of the small pile of First Year copies sitting on the coffee table in the sitting room below.

School could not have been quieter. Approaching the October midterm, everyone was exhausted and had already started to wind down. Next week, she would keep it light. There would no homework, not even for seniors who usually had an essay per week. Of course, she would set the Sixth Years some work for the break, but she wouldn't demand that they do it. Jane was conscientious, but not to an extreme. She was competent and diligent, but in no danger of dying under the weight of homework copies.

She often reflected on the woeful teaching she'd been subjected to during her school days. Her English teacher, Ms Hynes, had never risen from her seat. She would witter on about the state of students' handwriting, and how people misremembered quotations, such as saying, *Money is the root of all evil,* instead of *For the love of money is a root of all kinds of evil.* When someone wrote *should of* instead of *should have,* she nearly lost her mind and went on to lecture the class about the subtle tells in speech that reveal social class and level of education.

"Midterm tests," Claire said. Her mother loved to give the impression she knew exactly what was going on in all walks of life.

"Well, I'd better get started if I want to have my afternoon free." Jane sighed dramatically, before remembering her manners. "Oh, how was it? Did you win?"

"Of course not, Jane. I never win with batty Eileen as my partner. She's for the birds."

"Oh dear. Well, I hope—" Jane began.

"Listen, I've got to go. Talk soon." Having noticed an incoming call on her phone, or the shadow of a visitor behind the frosted glass window in the hall, Claire abruptly ended the call.

Jane was miffed. She took great care to bring their conversations to a natural conclusion, which was a courtesy her mother rarely repaid her. She laid her head back on her pillow and stared at the exposed beams overhead. She wondered again how best to respond to John's text message. She had kept him waiting long enough.

She tried to think of how someone who was popular with men would act in her shoes. The only person she could think of was Wendy Winters, the only other girl from her secondary school who had studied Arts in UCD with her. How would her old schoolfriend, the one who got invitations to three different debs on the same night, have handled this situation? She didn't like Wendy's style. Although men adored her; women didn't. Jane tried to think of a fictional character that she admired. There, too, she was at a loss.

OK, keep things simple, she said to herself as she stood up from her bed, feeling a sudden light-headedness that left her both disoriented and giddy. She sat back down. It had been a while since she'd had that sensation. She blinked her eyes several times, aware of an aura of flashing light at the corner of her right eye. *Oh, God, not a migraine.* She opened the bottle of sparkling water on her bedside locker. Picking up her phone again, she opened the second of the messages and typed in a cheery tone that did not feel like her own:

Hi John. Nice to hear from you. Wasn't sure if I was adding the right John Davy on Facebook. My Facebook page is in Arabic, so I have no idea what I'm doing! How are you? Still in London?

For some reason, whenever she logged in to Facebook on her computer, the default language was set to Arabic. She had to adjust it to English each time she opened it. But on her phone – which is where she had searched for John Davy's profile, discovered his single status and that he had a young daughter, sent him a friend request, and then cancelled it the following morning – all the settings were in English. She thought the bit about Arabic sounded light-hearted and comical, though. It was the kind of thing that might elicit a quick response.

Arabic? Oh, Jane, are you in the Middle East?

As predicted, his response was immediate. He must have been sitting with his phone in his hands. Could he have been eagerly awaiting her response?

No, that's the thing. I'm just not good at the Facebook.

She hoped to give the impression of a cavalier, devil may care Facebook user, who sent off requests for friendship like they were going out of fashion. Not that she wanted him to think she was lonely or desperate, but rather uninvested and indifferent.

Ha! So, what are you doing with yourself these days?

She hoped his eagerness to chat wasn't alcohol-fuelled. He could very easily be seated, alone and depressed, in a one-bedroom flat somewhere in the UK. She had slept way later than usual, and it was midday, but if John was an alcoholic he could already have had his first drink of the day or still be drunk from the night before. This line of thinking said a lot about the regard in which Jane held herself. Her automatic presumption was that if he was reaching out to her, he must have hit rock bottom.

Judging by his posts, it appeared that John remained a successful, handsome and wealthy man in his thirties, whose strong network of friendship and family provided a buffer from the temptations of daytime drinking and drug taking. His wife, whose photos featured very far back in his timeline, was a pristine, Asian-looking woman with strong cheekbones and a chin-length bob.

In her Facebook profile photo, she looked different – her hair had been lightened, and her eyes were an unusual mix of green and grey. She did not appear to be of Asian descent, after all. Her name was Liz Davy née Roberts. Her maiden name sounded very British. Her photos were set to public, and Jane could see all aspects of Liz's life, from her thirtieth birthday party to her parents gardening at home.

Both Liz and John described their relationship status as single on Facebook. Liz's features did not contort when she smiled. She was graceful and sophisticated, and much as Jane longed to find some fault, she had to conclude that John must be a complete idiot to have let her go.

Jane cast about for a witty response. Then, emboldened by the fact that he was the one seeking her out, she decided to let him wait. All those monotonous tasks that ate up her Saturdays – food shopping, window cleaning, meal preparation for the week ahead – became suddenly very doable.

CHAPTER FOUR
The Dress

Over the coming weeks, as Jane and John continued to exchange text messages, with Jane always being the one to end the conversation or to leave John hanging for a few hours, she became none the wiser as to his intentions. Afraid to have her dreams prematurely shattered, she had artfully dodged John's request to meet up in person until he suggested a Saturday night in late November, the exact date to be confirmed.

Margaret had proclaimed that, Saturday being a priority night, John must mean business. Jane's heart filled with joy at the thought that a man as wonderful and accomplished as John Davy would make her a priority in his life. Then again, Margaret tended to be unswervingly positive.

Jane had spent hours trawling the internet for a suitable dress. It had to be long, as she hated her legs – her thighs, in particular. If possible, it should have a high, shirred waist to lend the impression she was long-legged and elegant. Eventually she landed upon an outrageously priced Victorian dress from a vintage boutique on London's Marylebone Lane. It belonged to another time, but then, so did Jane. She feared that the dress might appear somewhat eccentric to John, whose girlfriends tended to be modern, city types.

When it arrived in the post five days later, her heart leaped for joy. She opened the box, eagerly loosening the tissue paper to reveal the exquisite pink ruffles at the collar, hem and cuffs. The green floral material was surprisingly light and soft against her skin, and the bodice fitted perfectly around her bust. As she caught a glimpse of herself in the full-length mirror, some curls escaped from the bun loosely tied atop her head. She wouldn't have looked out of place in a television period drama. The thought gratified and frightened her in equal measure. This aesthetic, she reflected, would most likely not appeal to the average man. John's tastes had always fallen somewhere safely in the middle, neither staid nor extravagant. It was a beautiful piece, and she had to keep it, even if it wasn't quite right for her first date with John.

Although they were in contact every second day, they had yet to speak on the phone. The end of November drew near, and Jane feared that their plan would never come to fruition. While she was petrified at the prospect of meeting him in person, even more terrifying was the possibility that this was for him – a recent divorcé – merely an experiment in escapism. If the situation that had somehow developed between them was drink fuelled, as she had initially feared, then she stood to have her heart shattered into a million pieces.

She felt strange about not having asked him how he'd gotten her number. It seemed awkward that he'd never explicitly mentioned having a daughter, despite there being so many photos of her on his Facebook page. At this point, the proposed date was still an amorphous idea, floating in the ether. Once she had tentatively agreed, he had never mentioned it again. She had pretended to have forgotten, which, she imagined, probably suited him quite well.

Her righteous indignation grew in steady increments until it had matured into a rage that pulsed through her veins. Doors she had always closed gently she slammed, with relish. The idle chatter of her students, previously a mere irritant, became a personal assault on her senses. John's most recent attempt at communication had been a text message on a Friday afternoon enquiring as to her plans for that night. She had left it resting unanswered on her phone with the intention of answering it on Monday. She hoped to pique his interest by making him wonder if she'd been out socialising at the weekend, if there wasn't some other successful, handsome man on the scene. The thought of this retribution sustained her over the following two days, allowing her to make it through what would otherwise have been an utterly miserable weekend.

That Sunday, at a quarter to midnight, her phone pinged from the depths of her bag. She had taken to keeping it at arm's length, to reduce the likelihood of her shooting off some impulsive message that she'd regret later. As she sifted through the contents of her large leather tote, her heart began to gallop, but she steeled herself for disappointment. It would, of course, be her mother or her sister – the former checking in; the latter looking for a favour. But to her delight, the sender's name was short, with an initial for his name.

So, Jane, we said we'd have dinner before the end of November! How would next Saturday suit you? Will you give me the pleasure of your company? J

It occurred to her that John hadn't given her much notice, and that this invitation had come from a place of fear. Perhaps he had sensed that his hold over her was loosening and felt compelled to reel her back in. Jane was aware that she read far too much romantic fiction for her own good, and that her expectations were not rooted in reality or informed by real life experience. If she wanted to have a relationship in the real world with a real man, she would have to drop her standards somewhat. But she wasn't going to hand herself over on a plate, either.

She turned off her phone. Feeling satisfied that the balance had been somewhat restored, she resolved to sleep soundly that night and respond at her leisure in the morning. She never had difficulty sleeping on nights like these – glorious times, when fate seemed to tip in her favour, as it often did in the lives of the heroines about whom she so fervently read. If anything, she wished she could stay awake long enough to delight in her victory, knowing only too well that it could be short-lived. She was glad that, despite her reservations, she had decided to hold onto the insanely expensive dress.

CHAPTER FIVE
Sisters

"I need you to be honest with me." Jane didn't usually discuss men with Charlotte, but she had to acknowledge her younger sister's superior knowledge in this arena.

"What, Jane? Spit it out!" Charlotte brought her cup of tea to her lips to conceal the grin tugging at the corners of her rosebud mouth.

"OK, so, if you were meeting up with someone you liked, but it was highly unlikely they liked you because they're out of your league, and there was probably a logical explanation for their contacting you, would you think it a bit desperate to wear a really beautiful dress?" Jane couldn't meet Charlotte's eyes, which were flickering with a mix of curiosity and delight.

Charlotte had never once doubted her attractiveness to the opposite sex. Their mother, not being quite pretty herself, tended to overvalue the importance of good looks. She would heap praise on her younger daughter without any regard for the feelings of her elder daughter.

"Excuse me, Jane," Charlotte said, clearly beginning to enjoy herself, "who is this man and where is the dress?"

The two sisters' personal styles were entirely at odds. Charlotte liked to keep abreast of the latest trends and was not averse to accentuating her more feminine features. Jane tended to favour conservative V-necks and Victorian collars. She had inherited her mother's slight bosom, and legs that she felt were far too short and heavy for someone her height.

"Oh, for God's sake, Jane, just show me the bloody dress already!"

Jane slipped into her bedroom and took the dress of her dreams from the hook on the back of the door. She presented herself to Charlotte with the dress draped awkwardly over the front of her body. She steeled herself against her sister's caustic tongue, almost afraid to look her fully in the eye.

"It's bloody awful, Jane. Not suitable for a date at all. It reminds me of something that Anne of Green Gables would wear. He'll just think you're weird. Who is it, anyway? Is he weird himself?"

Jane's cheeks flushed and her eyes welled up. All the hope she'd stored up over the past few weeks evaporated in an instant. She felt a surge of hatred, directed not only at Charlotte but at herself, for having trusted her sister with this most precious news. She ought to have known that Charlotte would always let her down by withholding praise or delivering a wounding remark. Had Jane, on some level, needed to be brought down to earth before she lost the run of herself? She had such a complicated relationship with pain. It almost felt good sometimes.

"Never mind!" Jane snapped. "You don't know him. I don't really know him, either. So, I guess that's not a contender."

She folded the dress and draped it over the back of the sofa. She brought her own cup of sweetened tea to her mouth, willing her sister to move on. Charlotte's visits were always fleeting. She chatted about work and relayed some banal stories about her inane friends before receiving a text message summoning her elsewhere. This time, her boyfriend had texted to say he was five minutes away. Heaven forbid he might have to wait a minute or two for her to gather up her belongings and use the bathroom! Ringing the doorbell, or coming in for a quick cup of tea, would be out of the question. He would sharply toot his horn, and Charlotte would glide out to the car, its engine still running, radio blaring loudly. Jane wondered why she bothered coming at all.

"Anne of Green Gables," Jane muttered. "I wish I had half of Anne's spirit."

Maybe John would like her dress, after all. It would be a test of his character. She was more determined now than ever to wear her period piece. And if he thought her weird, then good riddance! Jane's anger towards Charlotte served as a highly effective distraction from the nervous dread slowly spreading within her mind and her body. She was glad she had bitten her tongue and not divulged any more information to her sister, who would surely run to their mother with the news. At times, Jane considered the possibility that her sister hated her. Jane had never felt any jealousy towards Charlotte, who pitched herself so far above and beyond Jane in every respect that it seemed pointless to compete.

Jane rose abruptly and picked up both their mugs. She asked Charlotte whether Neil might like a cup, knowing full well that he wouldn't. Charlotte declined the offer on his behalf and made her customary bathroom visit to check her makeup and brush her hair before the bright lights of his BMW sedan flooded the sitting room. Jane busied herself in the kitchen to avoid Charlotte's forceful hug.

As children, they had gotten along for a while. She remembered their collective joy at Christmas, and a bout of shared enthusiasm for tennis in their preteen years, when they nursed the delusion that they would compete in Wimbledon one day and meet André Agassi. Charlotte had written her name alongside his on the inside cover of numerous Roald Dahl books, which Jane had read aloud to her at bedtime. Where had that sweet girl gone?

As soon as Charlotte had gotten a taste of popularity, she had abandoned Jane. Charlotte found her older sister an embarrassment – awkward around new people, invisible to boys. As she stood to gain nothing from her continued acquaintance with Jane, she disassociated from her sister when they were in school and out socially. Jane had been more embarrassed than hurt. It felt forced, awkward, and, most of all, unnecessary. Surely, Charlotte, who was so keen to make a good impression on her friends, would want them to think she was from a well-adjusted family. None of her friends blanked their own siblings in public.

One evening in her final year of school, as her father drove her home from a cinema trip with friends, Jane had told him that she saw Charlotte's behaviour towards her as a sign of low self-esteem. That afternoon, Charlotte had studiously avoided making eye contact as she walked by the window of the café where Jane sat with two friends. From the dramatic way in which Charlotte had suddenly twisted her head, as if to look over her opposite shoulder, Jane had known that her sister had seen them. Jane's father's silence had been a deafening reminder of where his loyalty lay.

It had been a difficult period in Jane's life. Her friendship circle had shrunk to a small group of girls who felt similarly inadequate around the popular set. Her best friend since First Year, Julia, had carelessly jettisoned her when the prospect of friendship with a more fashion forward set of girls loomed on the horizon. They were united in their fascination with the pre-debs – the practice graduation ball that would be held at the end of their penultimate year in school.

The most popular boys played rugby and were known by their surnames. She could recall their names without ever having laid eyes on them. She often felt tearful and nostalgic for the innocence of her early secondary school years. That was the time before everyone became obsessed with boys, drinking, and listening to the right type of music. How had the transition been so seamless for everyone else? She was terrified by the uncertainty and danger that came with being a teenager.

CHAPTER SIX
Jane Rebuffs a Friendly Man

Jane's features contorted in disgust as she gulped down her last mouthful of coffee. If she had not been in company, she would have spat out the last drop. Despite the bell having rung a second time, there were still a few small groups remaining in the staffroom. By now, they should all have been in their classrooms, taking roll call or distributing lesson notes.

Using the textbook alone, without providing supplementary notes or using a fancy PowerPoint presentation, was frowned upon in St Mary's. From very early on in her time there, Jane had known that appearances were every bit as important as the reality of what was going on in the classroom. Parents and students liked their children to be spoon-fed. As one might expect, a huge emphasis was placed on results in this exclusive girls-only day and boarding school.

"Not a fan?"

The young man's chirpy tone irked Jane. She had only wanted a shot in the arm before Sixth Year English, not an inane exchange about the quality of coffee from the staffroom's outdated machine. She avoided small talk if at all possible. It drained one's energy and consumed valuable time.

"Hmm, no!" She smiled weakly, without meeting the man's gaze.

She popped a wafer biscuit into her mouth to neutralise the bitter aftertaste.

"I don't believe it! Willy! What are you doing here?" Margaret opened her arms wide to the amiable-looking man queueing for the coffee machine.

He seemed equally surprised to see her. "I didn't know you were teaching here. How's Frank? I haven't seen him—"

"Since Niall and Brónagh's wedding!" Before Jane could slip away, Margaret turned and grabbed her arm. "This is Jane! Jane, this is Willy, Frank's friend from college. They were in the same class."

"Oh, really?" Jane wondered who was responsible for the unfortunate abbreviation of his name. "I'd better get going, Mags. Nice to meet you, William!"

She glanced at him before making a hurried exit. William appeared to be in his late thirties. He would have to be, if he'd been in Frank's class. He didn't pique her interest, but she presumed that his boyish, fresh-faced looks would be considered attractive by some women. If he was insulted by her hurried departure, he betrayed no signs of it. He continued to chat easily with Margaret about his reason for being at St Mary's on that chilly November morning.

Jane descended the stairs to the ground floor at pace. The staffroom was like a train station – you were guaranteed to meet someone new each day, whether or not you wanted to. Much to Jane's surprise, Margaret caught up with her by the time she'd reached the library.

"So, what do you think?" Margaret's eyes danced.

"Small talk!" Jane dramatically threw her eyes heavenward, making Margaret chuckle.

"He liked you, Jane," Margaret observed with a wry smile.

"No, he didn't. Who was he, anyway?" As Jane found such talk embarrassing, she tried to shift the emphasis to the man in question and away from any intentions he may have had in her regard.

"William de Barra. And he's single! First thing I checked," Margaret announced proudly.

"A bit too desperate for conversation for my liking." Whenever a man tried to gain her attention, she reckoned he mustn't be up to much.

"You're implacable, Jane. He's very handsome."

Jane had set her sights very firmly on John Davy. No friend of Frank's, especially not one called Willy, was going to distract her from her goal. Besides, John had their first date lined up for the coming weekend. If she were already appointing substitutes, how fickle would that make her?

"The handsome ones are the worst."

"Well, John Davy's handsome, isn't he?" Several students emerged from the library, and Margaret lowered her voice. "How come you're giving him a chance?"

"Well, in some instances, the very good-looking ones are the humblest. Look at those two ponces over there." Jane nodded in the direction of two language teachers, who were both gesticulating wildly so that everyone would know they were conversing in Italian. "I mean those two idiots wouldn't give us the time of day. If we threw ourselves at them at the next Christmas party, they'd be like—"

"Shush, Jane! Jesus. Message received. I get it, though. You're in the John Davy zone now."

Jane blushed deeply.

"Would you sleep with him on the first night, do you think, Jane? I mean it's not like he's a stranger. I mean, if things go really well?"

"Jesus Christ, Mags! To think you were censuring me a minute ago. I am not having this conversation on these premises."

But no one cared to listen. The schoolgirls were absorbed in their own drama, including unfinished homework and unrequited crushes.

"I just want to know what he wants from me." Jane let out a long and despairing sigh.

"Well, I think we both know what he wants," Margaret stage whispered as they parted company. Her classroom was in a different wing of the dusty Victorian building. "You just can't believe your luck!"

Jane took a deep breath before stepping over the threshold. Her classroom was a sanctuary, a refuge from her self-doubt and crippling fears. When Jane was at the helm – leading the discussion, guiding the girls through a text, teasing out their opinions – her mind was a calm and hospitable sea. For now, she was perfectly happy to leave her hopes, dreams, and all the potential heartbreak that might come with them, at the door.

CHAPTER SEVEN
A Date Is Set

Despite having made tentative plans to meet in Dublin city centre, Saturday drew nearer without any confirmation of the time or the location. Late Thursday night, John sent a friendly text suggesting that they meet at 8 p.m. at The Westbury, a luxury hotel just off Grafton Street. A flurry of messages ensued between the pair until well past midnight. Any doubt Jane might have had regarding his intentions were allayed when he expressly stated that he was looking forward to seeing her and signed off with an *X*.

That night, Jane drifted into the most beautiful slumber, which was cut short by the relentless percussion of rain on the weary roof above. When she examined her face in the bathroom mirror, her eyes were puffy, rimmed with red, and her complexion dry and blotchy. Her racing thoughts prevented her from falling back asleep, much as she longed for that fresh-faced, dewy look that only a good night's rest and a healthy diet could bestow.

After tossing and turning for an hour and a half, she rose from her bed and threw the curtains wide open. A shaft of glorious, golden light graced the foot of her bed. Momentarily tempted to try her luck again at recouping lost slumber, instead she headed to the kitchen to make herself a mind-blowingly strong cup of coffee.

***

Later that morning, Jane's orange Renault Clio and Margaret's boyfriend's black Volkswagen Golf arrived in the stony carpark at the same time. Jane's house was closer to St Mary's, and she often walked in the summer. Today was wet and windy, so she had chosen to drive. If she wasn't in her classroom a full forty minutes before her first class, she considered herself late and her day somewhat tainted by its imperfect start.

As Jane turned left towards her classroom, Margaret called, "What's up? Aren't you coming up for a coffee?"

It was their ritual to have a coffee in the morning. As much as Jane loved her students and her subject, the first class of the day was tough – you never knew what kind of reception you would get. By her own admission, she wasn't strict when it came to classroom discipline. On occasion, she'd had to rein in the ones who took a certain pleasure in testing her patience, and otherwise relied heavily on the students' goodwill, their respect for her, and their sense of propriety.

Jane shook her head. "I have a slew of copies to correct."

"I'll bring you one up, so?" Margaret kindly offered.

"And a few biscuits!" Jane paused, then added, "Please?"

"What else?" Margaret chuckled, striding in the opposite direction towards the staffroom.

Jane liked how her best friend knew her little habits. Each time Jane was home, her mother asked her how many sugars she'd like in her tea. And yet, Claire never forgot that Charlotte took one and a half teaspoons of brown sugar and a small splash of milk. Jane believed that this was not a conscious omission on her mother's part; it was an unconscious disregard, which was possibly much worse.

Jane thought of John Davy. She could not imagine him remembering little things about her – or anyone, for that matter. He gave the general impression of being forgetful, in a charmingly boyish sort of way.

Now, seated at her desk, Jane pulled the pile of copies towards her. She flicked through the first few and let out a sigh. Irish – her grandmother's first language, and the reason she had landed this job in the first place – was the downside to teaching at St Mary's. At first, she had been so grateful. When she graduated, while English positions were few and far between, there was a shocking lack of Irish teachers. She would have the pick of schools if she could reconcile herself with the idea of teaching the tenses on repeat for the rest of her working life.

Grammar was a drag, and her Irish was so rusty that she taught the classes as much as possible through English. After a year of a timetable dominated by Irish, with a sprinkling of English classes, the head of the English department retired out of the blue. Enid had reluctantly stepped up and assumed the role, and Jane had been given her first senior class ever. She was never quite able to shake off First Year Irish, though. Twelve classes a week, a penance.

On this particular Friday morning, she struggled to muster enthusiasm for the three classes that were scattered throughout her day. A miserable rain, the type that didn't clear for days, fell in sheets outside. It was enough to dampen anyone's spirits, even if you were due to go on a date with the man of your dreams the following night.

"Knock, knock!"

Jane hurried over to open the door for Margaret, who was standing with two mugs of coffee and a half packet of custard creams wedged under her arm.

"Thank you, Mags! I didn't get much sleep last night," Jane said. "How's Frank?"

Jane sometimes felt guilty at how her life dominated their conversation. She seemed always to be undergoing some form of emotional strife, whereas Margaret sailed through everything with aplomb.

"He's fine. Same as always." Margaret smiled.

She had always plumped for steady men. Although steady didn't always mean boring, in Jane's opinion it usually did.

Margaret was a constant and true friend. When Jane asked Margaret to accompany her to the Christmas party at the tennis club, and the squash instructor whose attention Jane had been trying to catch for months, even going as far as to sign up for private lessons, turned up with his girlfriend, no other friend could have rescued her from the pits of despair as Margaret had. Nor would any other person in this world have known better than Jane herself that she didn't even really like the man. Jane only wished she could return the favour more often.

Lost in her recollection, she hadn't heard a word Margaret had said. "Sorry?"

"Tell me about Saturday!" Margaret wore an expectant expression. "Have you two firmed things up?" Her eyes widened.

Jane couldn't help but feel pity for her friend, whose love life must lack passion. Frank had lovely dark eyes, and he adored Margaret in his muted type of way, but his masculine energy ebbed more than it flowed. "Yes! Oh God, Mags, I'm so nervous. He suggested The Westbury for eight."

"The Westbury? For a first date? I mean, start as you mean to go on, John Davy!"

"It's probably a bit sedate. Do you think? You kind of want a bit of background noise, a bit of energy?" Jane bit her lip, wondering if she should suggest a change of venue.

"Oh, now you're looking for things to worry about! Promise me one thing, though – Charlotte won't be doing your makeup!"

Jane groaned. The one and only time her younger sister had helped her get ready for a night out, she had applied Jane's eyeliner so very badly, dramatically veering from the lash line in places. Jane felt certain that she'd done it on purpose. "No! I'd never ask her again. I mean, her own make up is so perfectly applied and the one time she did mine, it was a disgrace. I was like Aunt Sally from – what's that programme with the scarecrow?"

"Worzel Gummidge. I know, right? And it's easier to put eyeliner on someone else than on yourself!" Margaret knew this only from the snatches of conversation she'd overheard in the staffroom from the younger teachers, who were obsessed with their eyebrows and with grooming in general.

"It was shocking. Do you think I should get it done professionally, I mean, by a makeup artist?"

"Oh, no. You don't want to feel as if the only way you'd be good enough for a date with John Davy is by getting professionals to work on you. I'd say you're better off not trying too hard, and not emotionally investing too much, either."

Jane was taken aback by this sudden U-turn. So far, Margaret had been her greatest supporter in this romantic adventure, and now she was advising Jane to manage her expectations.

"No, no – I don't mean to sound negative," Margaret said. "It's just, in my experience, things usually work out better when you don't go in wearing a ballgown like the one that Edel wore speed dating, remember? And then John's just sitting there in his Y-fronts."

Jane was not in the mood for funny anecdotes about former colleagues. "Ugh, Mags, I don't think the Westbury would allow it!"

"I don't know about that. They might insist upon it when they actually see how great he looks in them." Margaret smiled warmly, hoping she hadn't dampened Jane's spirits, but also aware that Jane was melodramatic and far too sensitive for her own good, and probably shouldn't be indulged in her rumination.

"I have got to go to choir," Margaret said, trotting off with one hand dramatically outstretched, as if she were performing on stage. "*Laaa*!"

Although she never had been openly criticised for her singing, Jane wasn't sure she would be an asset to the choir. As children, Jane and her sister sang along to songs in the back of their father's car, and their mother had lavished high praise only on Charlotte, causing Jane to fear she might be a crow. Jane had sought her mother's reassurance on this point on more than one occasion, but Claire Mythen had remained tight-lipped, which served only to reinforce Jane's doubts in this arena.

In the silence of her classroom, Jane pushed on with her corrections and readied herself for 1B Irish. After some time, she closed her eyes and tried to visualise herself with John. She just couldn't picture them together. Was it because she hadn't seen him in so long? Maybe this would change after their date on Saturday.

What would everyone in Glin say when they heard John Davy was dating one of the Mythen daughters? Everyone, including her own parents, would assume it was Charlotte. This thought caused Jane to sigh audibly. As the first two students entered her classroom, the sun broke through the clouds, bathing her classroom in a warm golden hue that made her feel that life was good and that she might not grow old alone, after all.

How fickle I am, she thought. *My mood changes with the weather.*

CHAPTER EIGHT
Pregaming

The gentle patter of rain against Jane's bedroom window eased her from a deep and dreamless sleep into wakefulness. She rose from her bed, remembering it was Saturday. This was to be the day that her life changed course. John Davy would declare his feelings for her, confessing that he had long admired her from afar. She couldn't bear to let herself enjoy this hope, for fear it would be taken away.

She rushed to the window and pulled back the curtains to catch her neighbour measuring the distance between their cars. Not even the crazy American could unsettle her today. Assuring herself that everything would work out for the best, she wondered how many drinks it would take to steady her nerves before leaving the house. She'd have to order the taxi now. In Greystones, they were few and far between.

As she lifted her phone from its usual resting place on the mantelpiece, she registered a missed call. Thankfully, it was not from John. It was Charlotte, asking a question about their joint bank account. Jane ignored it. Even though Charlotte knew full well that Jane would be going out on a much-anticipated date that night, it would never cross her mind to enquire as to how her sister was bearing up.

Charlotte lived in her own world and had been that way since an early age, never outgrowing the egocentric phase that Jane had skipped altogether. When their mother briefly stayed at a psychiatric hospital in Dublin due to her nerves, Charlotte had refused to pitch in at home and insisted instead on attending all the birthday parties and tennis club discos. Their father had been run ragged. Claire, who interpreted Charlotte's selfishness as a distress call, had capitulated to her every whim. Charlotte made friends easily but had difficulty keeping them. She was willing to go to war on the most trivial of matters, once sacrificing a five-year friendship over a book she had lent out, which was returned via the post in a dog-eared state. Jane knew her sister would never change.

Jane checked her phone. There was a text from Margaret, wishing her the best for that night, and one from John. Fearing that he might still cancel their date, she clicked on the message, her heart almost breaking through her chest. He was suggesting they meet earlier. This could mean he wanted to spend as much time with her as possible. The other, more likely, explanation was that he had gotten a last-minute invitation from a friend he hadn't known would be available.

She wondered whether she should insist she was available only in the late evening, to test the strength of his interest, but she had waited fifteen years for this moment. After exchanging a few more texts, they agreed to meet at seven. Jane tried not to let this last-minute tweaking of their plans affect the mood she was carefully curating.

Tonight was the night. In the worst case, John would declare his interest in Charlotte and ask Jane to act as his go-between; or, in the best case, meeting Jane in person would reveal to him the intensity of his true feelings and the two of them would exit the Westbury as a couple. For some unfathomable reason, the second scenario made her feel queasy.

Jane was determined to look her best. She fastened her hair in a messy bun, which emphasised her high cheekbones and swan-like neck, and applied minimal make-up. Blessed as she was with her mother's porcelain complexion, although her chin protruded a little too much for her liking and her nose bore a subtle bump, her appearance defied the conventional notions of beauty. Each of her features in isolation might have been considered unremarkable, but their combined effect appealed greatly to some.

In the end, she left the Victorian dress hanging in her wardrobe, opting instead for a simple pink dress and navy-blue ballet flats. The mirror reflected her quirky beauty, so that even she had to acknowledge it.

"I am beautiful. I am lovable." She shuffled the deck of affirmation cards. There had to be a better one – something that would make her feel hopeful but not presumptuous. The next card she selected at random depicted a naïve-looking girl with wide eyes and a foolish grin. "I find love at every turn."

Hoping to distract herself with something unrelated to the date, she dialled Margaret's number. Her call went unanswered, and eventually the dial tone timed out. As she started typing a reply to her sister's message from earlier, the taxi sounded its horn. Discarding the unfinished message, she took a deep breath. She gulped back the last drop of wine from her glass and braced herself for the thirty minutes of small talk that lay ahead.

As the evening sun cast a soft, amber glow upon the city streets, Jane marched towards the Westbury Hotel. A slight shift in the weather had transformed her outlook. The rain had cleared at some point during the taxi journey, just as they had passed that nice hotel in Stillorgan where her parents stayed when they visited each December. She felt an unfamiliar pang of nostalgia, and she knew it was the alcohol, but she didn't care.

Upon entering the hotel, she climbed the stairs, her heart fluttering with excitement. It felt as though she had lived her whole life in anticipation of this moment. And, as she walked towards the dark-haired man with a newspaper spread across the table in front of him, bowing his head in concentration, she knew that her heart was no longer her own. She could only hope that he'd treat it gently. At that moment, she knew it was a risk she was willing to take.

CHAPTER NINE
The One That Got Away

Jane felt weak at the knees. While far from the nervous ingenue she had been when they'd come close to their first kiss fifteen years before, she froze, unable to speak. Her hands trembled and her ears burned. She contemplated retreating to the bathroom to gather herself, but there was no guarantee that she would emerge with any more composure than she now possessed. She breathed deeply but was unable to remember whether the inhalation or the exhalation should be longer. She recalled listening to a podcast where a socially anxious neuroscientist had spoken at length about one method being invigorating and the other relaxing.

"Jane!"

Her frantic stream of thought ended abruptly, and John Davy came into focus, standing before her with an expression of genuine delight, extending his arms. He embraced her with such hearty enthusiasm that she felt immediately at ease. This boyish charm and easy manner were why John made friends everywhere he went. He made each person feel as if they were the most important person in the world.

This was how he had made Jane feel every time they had walked together across campus, chatted briefly in the library, or stopped to exchange pleasantries on the stairwell. The only time she had ever felt dispirited in his presence was on that day in the library tunnel, when he had seemed indifferent to her. Following that encounter, Jane had resolved to feign that same indifference whenever she bumped into him around Glin. This had occurred only twice, and on each of these occasions he had been accompanied by a different, exquisite-looking girl.

"Will you have something to drink? I can recommend the merlot." As he raised his glass, his hand was not as steady as she would have expected. Perhaps he, too, was feeling nervous.

"I'll have a whiskey sour. I'm sure they'll come over soon," she said.

An attractive waitress, who was hovering at the edges of various conversations in anticipation of a raised hand or a searching look, sashayed over to them. "Same again, sir?"

John shook his head and said, "Two whiskey sours, please."

The waitress slinked away.

John was seated on a soft plush sofa diagonally facing Jane's stiff armchair. She placed her hands on her knees, unsure as to what else she could do with them until her drink arrived. *Relax, relax, relax,* she told herself, aware her cheeks were already flushed. Remembering she had brought along a bottle of water, she rummaged in her bag.

Meanwhile, his eyes remained fixed upon her, and a knowing smile seemed poised to appear at any minute. She remembered how he had devoured her with his eyes that night at the party. He wanted her now, which meant he must have wanted her then. Her instincts had been right. But then, why had he treated her with such cool indifference the next time they had met?

"How have you been?" John asked, breaking into an unashamed grin, perhaps in acknowledgement of the strangeness of the situation.

It struck Jane that the two of them had never really known each other to start with. "Just dandy," she said, realizing she sounded almost flippant. She had never used this word before, but it conveyed nonchalance, at least. "How about you? What are you doing in London?"

"Just selling my soul." He lifted the almost-empty wine glass to his lips and tipped it, the last drops rolling slowly towards his mouth.

She looked away, as if she had caught him in an embarrassing act. Slowly and deliberately, he set the glass down. He repressed a belch, placing his hand on his stomach, and frowned. Jane considered leaving before he got any drunker. The waitress arrived and placed their whiskey sours on the glass table. Jane thanked the waitress, whose name badge read Irina. When John, who seemed not to register Irina's presence, reached for Jane's hand, she retracted it.

"You're drunk!" As she spoke the words, she realised how ridiculous she sounded. Her hand tingled. She could still feel his touch – a jolt of electricity, stunning her out of her self-righteousness. Her features softened.

"I'm sorry. I've had a few too many glasses of wine." He reached for her hand once more, and this time she allowed him to hold it.

What did it matter if he'd tried to take the edge off his nerves with half a bottle of wine? She, too, had tried to stem the flow of her own anxiety with alcohol. He released her hand and sat back against the floral cushion. The moment of intimacy passed, and they resumed being strangers.

"So, you have a daughter," Jane stated nervously, scanning his face for a flicker of annoyance or any indication she'd crossed a line.

He reached for his phone, which lay on the table between them, and scrolled through his photo gallery. "Yes, I do. Her name's Tilly. She's three." He reached across and showed Jane a girl whose face she instantly recognised.

"Oh! She's beautiful." Feigning surprise, she glanced from the photo to him and then back again, as if to discern a likeness between the two. Jane knew the child had her mother's features – widely spaced eyes, delicate button nose, full lips – but her coy smile, and the way she looked up from under hooded eyes, reminded Jane of a young John Davy.

"She's the spitting image of her mum. I don't know, sometimes I see myself in her."

"Yes! The impish grin."

Smiling, John placed the phone back down on the table.

"Do you just love having a daughter, or did you think you'd prefer a boy? Before she was born, I mean."

"Aw, you know," he said, "I did, I did. I thought I'd much prefer a boy, but girls are just so smart and funny." He shook his head in wonder. "And God, they are just so damn manipulative."

"Really? I like the sound of her. She must take after your mum. I always thought Paula Davy was a formidable woman."

"She'd be delighted to hear that. She always liked you, too."

Jane felt the blood rush to her cheeks. The compliment felt too much to bear, Paula was not easily won over. Jane looked down awkwardly at her feet, at a loss for words.

He chuckled. "She even wanted me to bring you to my debs." The snobby, implacable Paula thought her good enough to accompany her favourite son to the biggest occasion of his adolescent life, and yet John considered it comical.

"Well, she's cleverer than I thought, then," Jane snapped. Her annoyance seemed not to register with John. Why was it, she thought, that people insulted her so freely, as if her feelings didn't count?

"Oh, sorry! I didn't mean to say I—" he started. "I was an arsehole, Jane. I wanted some shiny showgirl—"

"That's OK, I never wanted to be a showgirl," she lied. Oh, how she had longed to be considered bright and fun.

"I didn't mean to upset you." John frowned. "It's just that you were so refined, and I was just your typical teenage boy."

She decided to change the subject. "What brings you home this weekend? Are you going to visit Clodagh?"

"God, no. I can think of twenty people I'd rather visit than my sister. Why? Are you and Clodagh good friends now or something?"

"Not at all." Jane frowned to convey disapproval at his disloyalty but felt all the more drawn to him.

She had never liked his prim and judgemental older sister, who was always asking Jane where she lived even though she knew that the Mythen family resided above their pub. This was during the years before they could afford to buy a family home. Jane had always sensed that Clodagh's snobbery was rooted in insecurity, but she never understood what made the local doctor's daughter so uncertain of her worth. She was attractive but unexceptional, clever but not scholarship material.

Jane had heard that Clodagh was now a consultant dermatologist and the second wife of an American entrepreneur. They had a vast house in South County Dublin, where they hosted extravagant parties and where Clodagh administered botulinum injections to family members and close friends who were too busy to attend her office during business hours.

"I'm here for you, Jane. You're the reason I came over," John teased, grinning smugly.

Jane was offended by his blithe indifference. Was the notion that anyone would make her a priority so farcical? John seemed to be too drunk to notice her irritation. This was not the same man she'd idolised all through college. The John she had loved from afar was self-assured and had no need to belittle anyone.

Perhaps his failed marriage had dented his confidence. He was certainly a lot heavier than when she'd last seen him swanning around Glin with a new girlfriend. His jawline had grown less defined, and his shirt was too tight across his chest. At thirty-seven, he had earned the frown lines that were etched into his forehead. The years had been kinder to her, but she had attended fewer parties, drunk less alcohol, and had much less fun.

He caught the attention of a passing waiter, pointed to their empty glasses, and nodded. A broad grin broke across the young Italian man's face, and he turned on his heel. Even men responded more favourably to John's charms than to hers. Without any prompting, John launched into a rambling monologue about backpacking in the Italian Dolomites with one of his ex-girlfriends. The sensible part of herself, to which she usually listened, felt a strong impulse to leave. She could stand up, make her apologies, and exit while the night was relatively young. The dream, as fanciful as it had been, would be over. But she froze, unable to move.

The waiter returned with their drinks.

"That's my girl," John told the waiter. "Jane and I were in primary school together."

The waiter feigned surprise and interest. Despite her embarrassment at her companion's inebriated state, Jane experienced a strange sense of satisfaction when he said her name.

"I'm very lucky that Jane has agreed to meet me," he mumbled, reaching for her hand for the third time that evening.

The waiter smiled awkwardly and wished them a good evening. As Jane allowed John's hand to rest awkwardly on hers, she felt no electric jolt. Still, she knew that her former self would have been impressed by the fact that John Davy had called her his girl. They continued sipping their whiskeys for a moment longer. With a sudden rush of inspiration, she reached for her bag. "Come on, John. We don't need any more drink. Let's go home!"

The bracing cold November night air gave John a second wind. His usual buoyant confidence restored, he stood up straight, with his hands buried deep in his pockets. She had forgotten how tall he was. Unsure as to how the rest of the evening would pan out, she busied herself with the buttons of her coat. It was only half past nine. Perhaps she had been too rash in suggesting they leave. Looking at him now, so strong and handsome, she felt protected from the wind and rain and all the other unfortunate things that life would surely throw her way.

She felt helpless in the face of her desires. Her fate was already sealed. As they walked past the Green in the general direction of the taxi rank, she was afraid that if either of them spoke, they'd somehow ruin everything. She vowed herself to silence, smiling sweetly as he periodically looked down at her.

"Jane," he began, and cleared his throat. He glanced down at his feet, visibly gathering himself, before meeting her gaze once more.

"Yes?" She willed him not to say the wrong thing.

"Well, this might seem strange. Or just creepy."

Her eyes widened, and she hoped his confession would not be the latter.

"I always liked you, you know! But I was to be introduced to someone's cousin and, well, she was the same type of girl that I always dated—"

Jane's cheeks flushed. "You felt like trying your hand at someone who wasn't conventionally beautiful. Wow!"

It wasn't the worst thing he could have said. Deep down, she had always known that she did not conform to the standard of beauty to which most men held women, but it was a disappointment, nonetheless. A man who had to think whether he found her attractive was not what she'd always dreamed of.

"No, no. Not at all. You are just as beautiful as any of the girls I've dated. I shouldn't be saying anything in this state. I'm very lucky you agreed to meet me. You're the one that got away."

Having shrugged off his earlier drunkenness, he now stood in the lamplight, declaring what sounded like some version of love. She had imagined a scenario just like this a million times.

"Are you hungry?" He offered the crook of his arm.

She took it. "Starving!" It occurred to her that she hadn't eaten anything substantial since lunchtime.

His hand gently touched the small of her back. They walked through the streets in search of a restaurant that would not require a booking, and landed, propitiously, at the door of a delightful Mediterranean-style eatery on Coppinger Row.

"This is us," he announced, holding the door open for her.

The other diners glanced up, first at him, then at her. They were an attractive couple, she guessed. She wished she could press pause. Nothing could improve on his earlier avowal of love. He had not used the word, of course, but he could not have spoken more earnestly or from the heart. They ate in companionable silence, as only long-married couples and very drunk people do.

When it came time to part, there was no need for words of reassurance. Jane had spent the most delightful evening of her life. There would be other nights of passion in their future. Their lips briefly brushed before he closed the taxi door. On the footpath outside his hotel on Stephen's Green he stood, waving, as the grey station wagon carried her off into the moonlight.

Nothing will ever be the same again, she thought.

She was right about that.

CHAPTER TEN
Charlotte's Announcement

Jane awoke from the soundest sleep of her life. It really had been a week of firsts. Her head, despite the excesses of the night before, was remarkably clear and calm. Unlike on most mornings, she had no appetite. She took this as a sign of contentment. Propping herself up against all the pillows and cushions on her double bed, she remained in a dreamlike state. She felt no need to retreat into the marvellous world of her imagination when her own real life had become so suddenly fulfilling.

John would be travelling home to Glin today and would surely need a good twelve hours before he was in a fit state to drive. Would he even have stirred by now? She longed for him to wish her a splendid day and express his hope that they could meet again very soon. John had bared his soul last night. The depth of his feelings for her had taken her by surprise. He had needed a considerable amount of Dutch courage to confess that she was the one that got away. Coming from anyone else, the expression would have made her cringe. She had spent many years measuring other men against him and finding them wanting; he had chosen women who would never compare to Jane. Balance had been restored.

A short, sharp beep summoned her from her reverie. She reached into the small oak locker where she had placed her phone before stumbling into bed. Much to her disappointment, the text was from her sister. Jane wasn't in the mood to meet Charlotte and her bullish fiancé, Neil, for lunch in a small café in Dún Laoghaire.

Charlotte was tolerable only in very small doses. Jane suspected that even her sister's inane friends, with their singular focus on smooth hair and gel manicures, found her self-absorbed and superficial. Charlotte loved to expound on the merits of radiofrequency microneedling and the preventative effects of Botox. She was fully absorbed in the culture of reality television, analysing and predicting relationship outcomes for couples on *90 Day Fiancé* as if her life depended on it.

Jane felt a tide of resentment rising at the thought of spending more than five minutes in Neil's company. Neil said very little but acted petulant if Charlotte failed to always include him in the conversation. He had retained the white-blonde hair of his youth, and his ruddy cheeks and permanent snarl gave the impression of a nasty cartoon character. To Jane, he had the look of someone who had spent too long in the bath.

When Margaret had asked her to clarify what exactly that would look like, Jane was unable to do so but said she felt his facial features were weak and unfinished, as if they'd been carved from a bar of soap by an amateur sculptor. Neil ran a Hallowe'en costume business that he'd inherited from his father. To his credit, he had made a huge success of the once-small family firm by taking it online at a time when his father preferred the idea of early retirement.

Grey clouds were gathering overhead. The sense of contentment with which she'd woken was starting to dissipate. Not even John Davy could rescue her from this mood. She applied her make-up, intermittently checking her phone. She pulled on an old floral dress, as she had no interest in making a good impression. Charlotte wouldn't notice how she looked, and Neil would make a silent inventory of all the things he disliked about her outfit, to share with Charlotte later during the ad breaks of one of their reality shows. At least, this is what she imagined he'd do, based on the way he spoke about his friends and family members in their absence.

When Jane entered the sushi restaurant, Neil jumped to his feet and pulled up a chair from a nearby table. He asked her what she'd like to drink.

"A green tea, please."

She caught a glimpse of her pale, milky face alongside Charlotte's in a mirror on the wall opposite. Her angular features appeared even more severe alongside her sister's softer profile. Was she any match for John Davy with his traditional good looks and natural charm? The whole idea seemed ridiculous now. She found it almost impossible to concentrate as Charlotte twittered on about how tricky parking was in the little side streets and how her sore throat wasn't responding to treatment with various homeopathic remedies. Charlotte was all the more tolerable when she had a few drinks on board, but she was studiously avoiding it during daylight hours of late.

The waitress appeared at their table. Against the backdrop of her sister's inane chatter, Jane wondered whether John would be attracted to this impish young woman in oversized dungarees and ankle boots. The young woman's skin remained crease-free when she smiled. Would being in a relationship with John Davy mean always comparing herself to other women and, invariably, falling short?

Meanwhile, Charlotte had moved on to a new topic: the film they were planning to see that afternoon. Charlotte and Neil had become avid cinemagoers in recent weeks, and now Jane knew why her sister had suggested meeting in Dún Laoghaire. The large multiplex cinema around the corner had been the pull.

"We have some news." Neil reached for Charlotte's hand across the table.

"It's a little unexpected." Charlotte looked to Neil, who kept his gaze fixed firmly on her, with little interest in Jane's reaction. "We're expecting a baby."

Jane was surprised that she hadn't joined the dots herself. They both awaited her reaction. She had no interest in having her own children or hearing about other people's. They were messy and inconvenient, and any parents she knew had lost all sense of their own identity. And yet, she knew better than to show any sign of this antipathy, instead reaching for an aspect of motherhood that interested her.

"Have you picked out any names?"

Charlotte and Neil exchanged a quick look.

"Milly for a girl, and Neill for a boy," Charlotte announced, squeezing her fiancé's forearm. "We're spelling it differently from Neil's name."

Parents who misspelled their children's names, whether through error or by design, were a major source of irritation for Jane. This had become a real issue in Ireland, where people added accents to vowels as they pleased. A child called Arran, a biblical name, could now be called Arán, which was Irish for bread.

"Have you told Mum and Dad, then?" Jane asked.

Charlotte looked at Neil and smiled her best Chesire cat grin. "We're driving down tonight and taking them out for dinner."

"Oh, that's wonderful." Her tone was flat. She wished she had injected a little more enthusiasm into her delivery, but neither Charlotte nor Neil seemed to have noticed. They were in their own bubble of contentment.

"Mum is going to be over the moon," Jane said. She made a note to keep her phone on mute for the next twenty-four hours.

When it came to children being born out of wedlock, their mother had not moved with the times. Claire's attitudes were as dated as her hair, which she still wore in the same style as she had when the girls were young. Jane could think of no better description for it than a layered helmet. Her mother would contact her for reassurance that this pregnancy was not unusual or a source of embarrassment. Jane would tell her mother what she wanted to hear: that it was fine, the norm, and nothing to worry about. After an initial spike in anxiety, Claire Mythen would slowly warm to the idea of being a grandmother, and they could all return to normal.

Jane wasn't sure what kind of mother Charlotte would make. Their mother had been emotionally distant yet solicitous; reserved yet consistent. Their father had been the warmer parent and would welcome them with open arms when they arrived home at the end of their college term. He would be a wonderful grandfather. Who knew, the role of grandmother might allow a softer version of her mother to emerge. As for Neil, she imagined he would relish the opportunity to stand at the sidelines on Saturday morning, letting the other parents know he was a past pupil of another rugby school, joking about not holding it against them, and generally irritating everyone.

Later, as she stood on the platform waiting for the less frequent Sunday train, her phone pinged. It was Margaret, inviting her to the cinema that evening. In an act of uncharacteristic spontaneity, she crossed the pedestrian bridge to the opposite platform and took the train to Dublin city centre instead.

When they emerged from the darkened theatre, Jane sneaked a

peek at her phone for the first time in about two hours. To her dismay, the closed envelope icon did not grace the screen on this occasion. It had taken every ounce of her willpower not to check her inbox before this point. How could John not have thought to leave a message, given that the night before had gone so very well? Perhaps his expression of romantic interest later in the evening had caused Jane to retroactively instil the preceding hours with an undeserved significance. In the past, a lukewarm farewell had prompted her to denigrate even the most delightful of encounters. She was just as likely to recast a miserable evening when a tiny glimmer of hope presented itself at its tail end.

John was likely back in the family home, being bombarded with female attention. He was the type that women, including his own mother and sister, never tired of fussing over. He had never had to court attention – there always was someone hanging on his every word. She could imagine her mother, her aunts, and even some of her emotionally buttoned-up friends, too, fawning over him at some point in the future.

"Everything OK?" Margaret's voice cut through her fantasy, bringing her abruptly back to earth.

"Oh, yeah! Don't mind me." She wished she could be the type to leave her romantic woes at the door. "I just can't stand the ups and downs of relationships. Not that I'm in one."

"Well, you could be. Very soon. Things move fast when you meet the right person."

Margaret's attempts to console her fell flat. Over the course of the past twenty-four hours, Jane had fallen from the heights of drunken elation to the depths of despair. Nothing had changed in the external circumstances of her relationship with John, and yet she was wholly disconsolate.

"So, what did you think?" Margaret enjoyed analysing films almost as much as she enjoyed watching them. "How do you think he came across?"

Jane struggled to recall much of what she had seen. Margaret had selected an interesting film, which appeared, at first sight, to appeal more to Jane's sensibilities than her own. It was an early showing of a documentary on the life of a revolutionary Irish psychiatrist. Jane later learned that he was a distant relative of Margaret's.

"He seemed warm enough in the interviews. Though probably not a great family man."

She had spent the previous two hours rerunning the scenes of her own drama, wincing at the memory of their drunken stroll up Grafton Street, but heartened by the very pleasant few hours they'd spent eating cheese and sipping white wine before parting company. When she tried to recall the content of their conversation, she could retrieve only snatches of it. They both had been very drunk by the night's end.

Sensing that Jane's mind was elsewhere, Margaret abandoned any hopes she'd had of discussing her mother's relative and his revolutionary work. She hadn't pushed for information about the date, as it clearly had not gone to plan. Jane's eyeroll and muted sigh had conveyed to her that the subject of John Davy was better left untouched. Still, Margaret knew that Jane was prone to pessimism when it came to her love life.

"Was it really all that bad, Jane?"

"Worse, Mags! Well, I thought it had gone well until today. He hasn't texted or called."

"Oh, well, you know the day isn't over yet. Don't give up hope! It's more a case that today has not gone so well."

Jane turned off her phone and vowed not to switch it back on until the following morning. She would rather bury her hopes than stoke the flames of disappointment. "Let's go for a drink," she proposed, with forced cheer. "Bar food is fine with me!"

"OK. We can pick apart the date—"

"Let's not! I'm so tired of men and their unpredictability. I've had it with them." Jane tugged her friend in the direction of a hotel bar, unsure if there would be anything more substantial on the menu than salted snacks, the distant memory of a martini drawing her in.

The two women settled themselves at the bar. Jane perused the cocktail menu, as if she hadn't already chosen.

"What am I doing wrong? If someone told me that some man they'd had a huge crush on as a teenager had contacted them out of the blue, after years of zero contact, and they were going on a date, I'd think they were delusional. Wouldn't you?" Jane searched her friend's face for her true reaction.

As always, Margaret was inscrutable. Her expression remained composed, and her habit of pausing before speaking gave her ample time to formulate the most diplomatic answer. "Well, no, I don't see it like that. He's probably visiting his parents. You only saw each other last night. I'm certain he'll call, Jane. I mean, you don't contact someone after fifteen years on a whim. Something prompted him to get back in touch."

"I still haven't asked him how he got my number."

"Why not? It's a pretty straightforward question. Nothing unreasonable in wanting to know," Margaret said.

"I don't know. It just feels awkward. I feel like I'm pretending to be this worldly person, who isn't that bothered about the minutiae of whatever this is. If I start asking him for all these details, it might break the spell."

"Anyway, what does it matter? He probably got it from a mutual friend."

Her spirits were lifted by her best friend's soothing words and the warm feeling at the base of her throat following her first sip of hot whiskey. Margaret was deep in conversation with the barman, having seamlessly transitioned from banal small talk about the weather into a meaningful exchange about the young man's daughter. Jane smiled to herself, absently plucking her phone from her bag. She was about to power it on when she remembered her resolution and pushed it back down out of reach under her Moleskine diary. She cast her eyes around the sparsely populated bar.

A few girls at a high table tittered in unison. They were heavily made up, and had the kind of long, poker-straight hair that only women with perfectly shaped heads and small, pretty faces could pull off. They spoke loudly and without inhibition, seeming keen to capture the attention of the two men sitting at the opposite end of the bar. Jane looked over at the men. One was reading a newspaper, and the other was looking straight at her.

She quickly looked away. Jane wasn't used to receiving male attention. She glanced back again. It was the man she had met by the coffee machine in the staffroom a few days earlier. Although she hadn't found him attractive then, now she had to admit he was quite handsome, in a boyish way. She'd always preferred men to boys.

"Mags!" she hissed. "Don't look now—"

Margaret immediately turned her head.

Jane gently prodded her arm. "Jesus, Mags! Could you be less discreet? It's Frank's friend."

Margaret attempted to discreetly look over her shoulder. "Oh, it's William," Margaret blurted. William overheard her and took it as his cue to walk over to them. "Jane, this is your weekend! You've turned into a man magnet!"

Jane was quite sure he wasn't her type. For one thing, he was too eager, which she read as a sure sign of desperation. "Stop it," Jane whispered conspiratorially.

"I'm just excited for you!" Margaret grinned with the air of a naughty child who knew she wouldn't be punished.

Margaret had a complete lack of interest in any men other than her partner. Jane wanted that for herself. She knew that if she were in a relationship with John Davy, she would never look at or think about another man. Margaret effortlessly hopped down from her stool and hugged William, who acknowledged Jane with a nod and a smile. Again, Jane noted his boyish good looks.

"Frank will be raging he wasn't here," Margaret said.

Jane doubted that. Frank was a dour type who was rarely overtaken by feelings. Margaret waved to the barman for another round, grinning so widely that Jane wondered if she could already be drunk. She was regretting her suggestion that they skip dinner. She had wanted a sympathetic ear, not some crazy wing woman who would give this man the impression that Jane was interested in him. Margaret and William began talking shop and Jane tuned out, catching only the occasional reference to drains or roadworks.

After some time, Margaret turned to Jane and said, "They're going to CPO a section of the grounds, Jane!"

"No, no!" William laughed. "We're working on the road outside, but we will need to take a little bit of St Mary's. We're upgrading the roads in the area."

Jane nodded, wondering if there could be a conversational topic less to her taste.

"Ah, so you were schmoozing Babs, then?" Margaret said to William. "Trying to get her to sign it over."

Jane knew that this ineffectual creature would be no match for the maneater that was their headmistress, Barbara.

"Oh, no. I don't think there will be any schmoozing needed. It's a pretty routine procedure. We'll make an offer—"

"You clearly don't know Babs!" Margaret tittered, lifting her wine glass clumsily. She got up and adjusted her skirt before excusing herself. "Back in a sec. Just going to powder my nose!"

"I have a niece called Jane, after my granny." William seemed more at ease now.

"Ah, how nice." Jane smiled weakly, keeping her language and tone as neutral as possible to discourage any further disclosure on his part.

"Can I get you a drink?" William turned to beckon his friend, who studiously avoided his gaze. "Michael!"

"Michael doesn't seem to be in a sociable mood." Jane was eager to wrap things up. "Well, I'll let you get back to him. Margaret and I must discuss something about work for tomorrow. A presentation. We're here to work, unfortunately."

If William was offended, he gave no obvious sign of it. He wished her luck and excused himself. They parted company on good terms, their dignity intact.

When Margaret returned from the restroom, she was surprised to see Jane sitting alone. "What happened?" she asked, plonking her bag on the bar.

"Nothing. He went back to his friend."

"Oh, OK," Margaret said, rolling her eyes, "I hope you were friendly, Jane."

"Of course. Now, what were we saying? You think I shouldn't give up hope."

"Give up hope!" Margaret guffawed, slapping her hand on her thigh. "You're so dramatic. He's at home with his family in Limerick, not lost at sea!"

Margaret had a knack of bringing everything into perspective. Jane had been awfully foolish. There was still hope. She glanced over at the other end of the bar and noted that both men had left. The coven of flaxen-haired girls at the high table were discussing where to go next. Jane caught the barman's eye and signalled for another round. *To hope,* she thought, *that little thing with feathers!*

CHAPTER ELEVEN
A Call from Home

Upon arriving home from the bar that night, she went straight to bed without checking her phone. When she awoke on Monday morning to discover that John had still not bothered to call or text, the anger she felt was invigorating. She plotted her revenge with gleeful precision. If, eventually, he ever did get around to phoning her, she would not accept his call. She would wait seven days before issuing a sunny and casual reply that conveyed the true extent of her indifference.

Meanwhile, Jane anticipated her mother's inevitable phone call about Charlotte's news with a sense of dread. With each passing hour, her frustration with John grew in inverse proportion to her shrinking tolerance for her mother. By Friday evening, she was ready to strangle one or both of them.

On Saturday morning, when her mobile trilled from the pocket of the dressing gown she had slung carelessly over the bedpost the night before, Jane was suddenly mobilised by hope. Jumping from her bed onto the cold hardwood floor, she stubbed her toe against the bedframe as she reached for her phone. If the call was from John, it would all be worth it.

No such luck. Her mother's name flashed on the screen. Feeling headachy and slightly hungover from the half bottle of wine she'd polished off the night before, she was tempted to repair to her bed for the rest of the morning. It was only nine o'clock. When the call timed out, she briefly considered putting her mother off for another few hours, but she knew sleep would elude her. She touched the appropriate button on the screen and waited for the call to connect.

Her mother picked up within two rings. "What do you think of your sister's news, then?"

"Oh, it's great. Isn't it?" Her tone was flat and lifeless. "Are you delighted yourself?"

"Well, I am. We are both delighted for the pair of them."

"Of course! It will be wonderful for them." Jane contemplated faking an incoming call.

"She will be a very good mother. She's always loved children."

Jane questioned the accuracy of this statement. Charlotte spoke with bitterness and rancour about Neil's many nieces and nephews. She had nicknames for them all, with a particularly cruel one for the eldest boy, who had a pronounced underbite.

"She's already thinking of names," Claire continued. "Your father, well, you know he's not a man of very many words, but he is—"

"Delighted? Thrilled?" Perhaps by finishing her mother's sentences, she could expedite this tedious conversation. "He must be so excited!"

"I mean, she would love a girl. And I think it would suit her to have a girl. She'd just love everything about having a little girl, all the beautiful—"

"Clothes! I know, the dresses!" Jane thought she might as well turn it into a game.

"She is so good with children. You should see her with Neil's—"

"Nieces and nephews! I know, she is great with them. Well, I'm delighted for her." Eager to change the subject, Jane asked, "Any snow in Limerick?"

"No! Why?"

"It's looking like we might be having plenty of snow down here this Christmas."

Claire Mythen tutted loudly. "You make sure that principal allows you to finish up early, so you can get home safely this year. It was a near-disaster last year, with you driving on those icy roads on Christmas Eve."

"Oh, I will," Jane said, knowing full well she would never dare ask for special treatment from Barbara.

She had no desire to make herself beholden to her needy, self-serving headmistress, whose generosity extended only to the male members of staff. As Claire went on to air all her latest grievances and anxieties, Jane listened, but without her usual equanimity. Knowing full well that any advice or sage words she proffered would not be heeded, she generally tended to make sympathetic noises and agree with whatever her mother said. Today was different.

CHAPTER TWELVE
A Welcome Distraction

As Jane entered the majestic, high-ceilinged drawing room that now functioned as the staffroom of St Mary's, a suspicious silence enveloped the space. Ordinarily, the sharp change in atmosphere would have alerted her to the possibility that she was the subject of gossip, but Margaret's presence among the teachers huddled around the fireplace was an immediate source of reassurance. No one would dare speak ill of Jane in the presence of her most loyal companion.

Jane liked to say she was not fond of gossip, but the truth was that she thrived on speculation, preferably of the harmless kind. Pretending that her curiosity had not been piqued by the conflab, Jane went through the motions of making her usual morning coffee, rinsing her mug, and looking around absently for the carton of milk, which had been left open on one of the large round tables. She was relieved to hear the loud whispering resume and gather pace, punctuated with Margaret's distinctive snorts of laughter. It was only a matter of time before she would be summoned to partake in the gossipmongering.

As she patiently stirred in a third spoonful of sugar, the door swung open. An uncharacteristically unkempt Barbara Canning leaned her full weight on the door handle, exclaiming in a distinctly disgruntled voice, "Bell's rung, ladies and gentlemen!"

Barbara was not the type of headmistress you saw roaming the corridors. While some accused her of not knowing the student body particularly well, Jane had the impression that Barbara was overly familiar with a core group of Sixth Year girls. She treated them as friends, rather than students. There was a constant stream of senior girls going in and out of her office to complain that their lives had been inconvenienced in some manner or other by a member of staff. Jane was glad that she had established herself as a strict but fair teacher under the previous head. Carmel Fitzgerald had been an unwavering source of support for all staff members, old and new. Barbara was divisive, particularly amongst the female teachers.

Jane was far too reserved to ever qualify as a potential friend for Barbara, a somewhat overpowering woman in her late fifties with boundless energy and a wonderful capacity for laughter. Her husband, JP, was one of the leading solicitors in Wicklow town. They lived near the train station in a beautiful, detached house, where every year they hosted Christmas drinks for the staff of St Mary's, her husband's secretary, and a handful of associate solicitors from his practice. No one would ever want to miss one of these bashes.

Margaret and Jane knew to keep their distance whenever Barbara had a new man in her sights. Each year she selected a new target, usually someone whose wife or girlfriend had recently dumped him for someone richer or better looking. This year, she was obsessed with the young substitute French teacher, Henri. JP could not have been less concerned. The pretty and ambitious solicitor who had recently joined his firm had completely absorbed his attentions at the last holiday party.

Jane waited for Margaret in the staffroom's kitchenette, dramatically raising her eyebrows.

"Looks like the stress is getting to someone," Margaret remarked, nodding in the direction of the door, which slammed back loudly on its hinges. "I'll fill you in later."

Jane could contain her excitement no longer. "Tell me now! Let's talk as we walk."

She carried the coffee mug close to her chest behind a copy of that day's newspaper. Barbara's secretary, Ger, had taken to standing outside her office, watching closely as the teachers proceeded to the stairs. Several weeks ago, Barbara had asked her to keep note of those teachers who smuggled hot beverages out of the staffroom. It had been Barbara's intention to address the concern with the individuals in question on a one-to-one basis. Ger, no stranger to conflict, directly confronted the teachers with a short, sharp reminder that they were in breach of a recently imposed school rule. Today, there was neither sight nor sound of the small, freckled middle-aged woman. Jane and Margaret peered through the glass panel in the office door at her empty chair.

Margaret nodded in the direction of Barbara's office. "She's needed elsewhere this morning." Margaret looked over her shoulder to catch the eye of another teacher, who chuckled in acknowledgement of the shared joke. "I couldn't do the story justice if I told it to you now. Far too much to tell. I'll call in at break."

Temporarily distracted from agonising over her love life, Jane's spirits were buoyed by the hope of a school-wide scandal. Although even the most salacious gossip would not change the fact that her romantic prospects had flatlined quite unexpectedly, it was better than nothing. The first three classes were more painful than usual, on account of the classroom being freezing cold. Housekeeping, no doubt under Barbara's instruction, had timed the heating to switch on a mere hour before school commenced. A building of this age, with such capacious classrooms and drafty corridors, required many hours to heat through.

Being a cold creature, Jane would often lean against the radiator during class with her back to the students in the depths of winter. This morning, she put down roots at the back, hoping the heat would have an invigorating effect. At various points during the morning's lessons she found herself on the verge of drifting off to sleep. Margaret's short, sharp knock on the door a few minutes after the bell for morning break roused her from her reverie.

"This had better be good," Jane said. "I am in the doldrums this morning."

"Oh, believe me, this is better than you could ever imagine."

Jane doubted this. The only thing that could bolster her spirit on this day would be the arrival of John Davy at her door, bearing flowers and an abject apology.

"Go on, then. Take my seat." Jane remained at the back of the classroom, as Margaret adjusted the swivel chair more graciously than Jane could ever manage.

"Well, who's the least likely man on the staff to have an affair?"

"What? Seriously, Margaret? You are not in possession of gossip as juicy as that!"

"I'm pretty sure I am." Margaret was not prone to wasting anyone's time, least of all her own, with silly jokes. "You know me. I wouldn't make things up."

Jane briefly considered this and determined it to be true. "Crikey. Don't tell me now, I want to guess." Jane trawled through the departments, starting with English. "English: no men. Irish: no men. French: those two plonkers are all talk. So, we're looking for a goody-goody, then?"

"Yep, keep going. Someone you'd never suspect." Margaret was bursting to tell, but she would not deny Jane the opportunity to guess. Her best friend loved nothing more than solving a mystery. She would have made a wonderful Miss Marple.

"OK, eh. Is it John Paul, the PE teacher? He's hardly squeaky clean, though. I mean, he loves himself, and he thinks all women find him irresistible—"

"Nah, this man is not someone you'd ever suspect."

"Let me see. A teaching member of staff, right? Full time?"

"Yeah, yeah. Well, I'm not sure if they're school or department paid, but they're well-established and respected."

"Jesus, don't tell me it's Robert O' Leary. I mean, I will lose all faith in humanity—"

"No, it's not Robert. You're right, he would be very unlikely to cheat on his wife."

Robert taught geography and was the loveliest man. Respected by teachers and students alike, he had been married to Elaine, the former librarian, for twenty-five years and their relationship was widely acknowledged as something to aspire towards. Both their daughters had attended St Mary's.

"Thank God for that! So, who's the cheating bastard, then? No, don't tell me. I really want to guess. I'm not going anywhere near that staffroom until I've figured it out, someone will blurt it out. Promise me you won't tell me!"

"Oh, it's good to have the old Jane back." Margaret sat back, interlacing her fingers as she watched her friend's mouth twitch from left to right.

Jane continued her process of elimination. Suddenly, her eyes widened, and a grin tugged at the corners of her mouth. "Oh my God. Not Rossa Delaney?"

"Yessiree!" shouted Margaret.

The first bell sounded in the corridor outside.

As Margaret stood up, Jane ran to the door and held it shut. "You're going nowhere until you tell me the details, and how we became privy to this news."

Margaret giggled. "I'm going to leave you to solve the second part of the puzzle! Who did he have the affair with?"

"We know her? She works here?" Jane spotted the diligent students gathering outside, the ones who spent the break packing their bags and reading over their notes from their previous lesson.

"OK, OK," she said, releasing her grip on Margaret's forearm. "Go, go! But call back in here at lunch. You're on late lunch today, right? Oh, damn it, I'm on early lunch."

"I'll call in. I have a double fifth later, but I'll give them a break halfway through."

"Can you give me a clue? But don't make it too obvious."

"You're putting me under too much pressure now!" Margaret laughed.

She opened the door and an earnest looking Second Year student, carrying her rucksack on both shoulders, stepped gingerly into the classroom. With that, Jane and Margaret's conversation came to a natural end.

It was the first time in weeks that Jane's mind had lingered on any subject apart from John Davy. While a very sensible part of herself wished she had never heard from him that fateful day in late October, an even more tenacious part could not relinquish the hope that he would re-appear with an acceptable reason for his absence. For now, she was pleased to dwell upon the delightful subject of Rossa Delaney and his wandering heart.

It was hard to keep her mind on Fifth Year English. She'd had to interrupt a heated debate on the topic of Kris Kindle presents. Alison Hampton, who was one of the more outspoken members of the class, condoned abandoning the custom they had started in First Year, as a much smaller form class of only fifteen girls, seeing as they were no longer really a unit. Apart from roll call (which took only ten minutes) and English (the only core subject that was not streamed according to academic performance at senior level), they had no other classes in common and were now a disparate group. It was a controversial opinion and her use of the word *disparate* had alienated some of the less bookish girls, who immediately sided with Caroline Mitchell, her chief opponent on this matter. Jane's favourite student, Brid, the mousy daughter of two serious academics, had no opinion on the matter. Jane admired her sheer apathy.

When Jane had finally captured the students' attention with talk of the Christmas test and the poetry that might appear on the paper, she was suddenly reminded that she hadn't actually set the paper in question yet. It would be the first time since Daniel had unceremoniously asked her for a divorce that she had dropped the ball. It was a habit of hers to have all examination papers set, printed, spell-checked, stapled, and filed in the secretary's bottom drawer at least two weeks before the testing period began. This glaring omission was, of course, due to her recently developed obsession with John Davy.

She made a note in her diary to start selecting questions from past examination papers at lunchtime. Perhaps this distraction was just what she needed. As the bell rang and the girls filed out of the room, with Caroline holding forth on the merits of Kris Kindle and the joy of Christmas, Margaret appeared.

"Oh yes!" Jane said. "I'm not taking lunch today. I've got to set the bloody Christmas tests so I could do with a bit of that scandal."

Bríd was still packing up her books, copies, and coloured pens. She and Margaret exchanged a quick glance. Jane knew that she was not the type to pass on anything she overheard to her peers. Nonetheless, she waited until Bríd had left the classroom before continuing her interrogation.

"OK, so as I said," Jane began, "you don't give me any clues unless I ask for them, right?"

"Of course." Margaret settled into the one comfortable student chair in the room. It was usually a case of first come, first served, but Jane occasionally offered it to the student who had outperformed all others in a recent class test or had apprised her of some interesting, obscure fact she would never otherwise have known.

"Now, you can only answer yes or no!"

"Deal. Now, come on, I've only given them a short break," Margaret reminded her. She'd ordered her students to wander the corridors for five minutes halfway through Double History.

Jane drummed her fingers on the desk as she silently worked her way through the alphabet, eliminating potential suspects. She paused and wondered whether she ought to double-check that it was a member of the teaching staff. There were so many women employed at St Mary's in a part-time capacity: special needs assistants; cooks; the woman who came in to do flower arranging with Transition Year on Tuesdays; the freelance basketball coach who worked at several schools in the area.

There was one mother whose occupation seemed to change

with the wind. When her daughter's French examination was marked incorrectly one year, she came in to meet the principal as a former French teacher. When her younger daughter was going on a ski trip to France, she volunteered to chaperone as she happened to be a former semi-professional skier whose career was derailed by an injury. There was talk amongst the male staff of her having worked as a runway model. Or was it that they thought she was good-looking enough to be one? Hadn't the science teacher, Pat Delahunt, commented that she should be doing Pilates on a catwalk rather than just teaching it? Sure, she was tall and slim, but her features were unremarkable, and the corners of her mouth turned downward, giving the impression she'd just tasted something bitter. It was also hard to overlook the teeth, some of which were capped, creating a step-like effect between the original, untouched ones and those carefully prepared in some fancy dental lab on the Southside of Dublin.

Margaret assured her that the woman in question was, indeed, a full-time, permanent member of staff and they both knew her very well. When she landed on *K*, as none of the teachers' first names began with this letter, she swiftly switched her attention to surnames. Just as she was about to progress to *L*, certain the offending party was to be found further down the alphabet, she landed on *Killeen*. Suddenly, everything slid into place.

"Oh my God, it's Cathy Killeen. Happily married Cathy!" Jane spoke these words in utter disbelief.

And yet, it made sense in retrospect. Naturally, it was going to be someone with a perfect home life, and an adoring and affectionate husband who was low on masculine energy. Jane had met Paul on several occasions, and he was decidedly wimpy. She had witnessed the endless photos on Facebook of them casting votes in referenda, marching in solidarity with minority groups, their children in buggies and their faces painted in support of the cause.

Cathy was the girl next door that most men found attractive, even if she wasn't their type. The worst part is that Cathy and Rossa had made no effort to hide their affection for each other. They flirted so openly and obviously that everyone assumed there couldn't be anything going on between them. Their respective spouses socialised at staff parties and gravitated towards each other at Sports Day, chatting awkwardly as Cathy and Rossa joked about.

Beaming, Margaret got to her feet. She had no need to confirm Jane's answer. What surprised Jane most was that a few of the teachers who had huddled around the fireplace in the staffroom, visibly taking pleasure in the salaciousness of the tale, were Cathy's friends. Yes, Nessa Doyle and Laura Gethings had the potential to be somewhat bitchy, but Margaret and Cathy were both members of the history department. This was the most harmonious of all St Mary's departments, and it was widely acknowledged that this was due, in no small part, to Cathy's leadership.

Had it been the librarian, Róisín, who huffed and puffed over the smallest of student transgressions, such as someone returning a book with earmarked corners, Jane could have understood their shared glee in discovering her indiscretions, but Cathy was thoughtful, and easy to work with. When Margaret, whose role it was to oversee the running of Christmas and summer exams, had taken ill unexpectedly last May, some of the other staff members, including Jane, had volunteered to divide the week-long duties amongst themselves. Jane couldn't sleep at night; such was her worry about misreading the timetable or dismissing a class too early from the exam hall. Intuiting her anxiety, Cathy had made sure to pop in every time Jane was scheduled to administer an exam. She came in early and helped Jane to rearrange the seating and distribute exam papers. Jane wondered now why they hadn't become friends.

The classroom remained empty. Jane repeatedly checked her watch. After a while, she thought to check her timetable, which she had carefully sellotaped to the back of her teacher's journal. She had forgotten that she had a free period after lunch on Monday afternoon when everyone else was back in class. When she got to the staffroom, it was deserted. She grabbed some crackers and cheese, and a yogurt from the fridge. Spreading that day's newspaper across the lunch table, she felt that life could still be good without John Davy. There was nothing like a few First-Year classes back-to-back on a Monday morning to make you really appreciate your lunchtime. The world had taken on a positive hue.

Just then, a man cleared his throat abruptly on the far side of the staffroom door. The gold door handle turned a fraction, as if someone was contemplating entering but had been delayed by a conversation outside. A medley of hushed voices ensued. One was light and the other gravelly. The handle turned abruptly and Rossa Delaney walked in.

Jane's cheeks flushed, in surprise at seeing him so soon after the news had broken. As she felt the heat moving down her neck, she cast her eyes quickly to her décolletage. It was flaming red. Rossa nodded in his usual reserved way that could easily be mistaken for arrogance but which she knew by now to be shyness. In fact, she had thought him truly awful when he had started as a young maths teacher five years earlier. She had slowly warmed to him as she saw evidence of his wry sense of humour. Would it be suspicious if she didn't engage with him at all as he stood at the water cooler, filling up a Star Wars flask that must belong to his son?

The door opened again. In her inimitable way, Barbara Canning leaned into the unlit room with her full weight on the door handle. She flicked on the lights in a way that made Jane feel she had been remiss by sitting in the dark, before uttering Rossa's name. Seeming somewhat preoccupied, she did not acknowledge Jane. Rossa grunted, but not in an unfriendly way. He left, with his flask only half-filled, to follow the headmistress down the stairs to her office. Rossa's phlegmatic response surprised Jane, and she wondered if there had been a gross misunderstanding on Margaret's part.

It occurred to her that not so long ago she had been the subject of such gossip, albeit as the person who was being cheated on. It had been a dark period in her life, and although the wounds had closed, they might never fully heal. She did not love Daniel anymore, but the shock had never left her. Her greatest loss incurred was that of time. Her entire twenties had been a lie. Even the happy moments she and Daniel had shared – presuming he had been happy during those times – had led up to his ultimate betrayal. The hardest part was that he and Hillary were still together. Even their refusal to marry would seem to suggest that they viewed their relationship as being superior to his brief marriage to Jane.

If Daniel had not fallen deeply in love with his younger associate, would he still be married to Jane? She believed he would, and that she would be mildly happy, with a few small children. Though not particularly suited to motherhood, she would nonetheless be delighted to have borne his children. They would be mathematical, musical and blonde, like him. Two girls and a boy, all three skinny and long-legged. Sometimes she dreamed of them. But when she awoke to her present reality, she was invariably flooded with a sense of relief.

CHAPTER THIRTEEN
Spiralling

A week had gone by, and John Davy had neither called nor texted. Wherever he was, and whatever he was doing, his mind was not on Jane. She played The Smiths on repeat, losing herself in their haunting lyrics and plaintive melodies. She watched intense Nordic crime, taking strength from the way the female lead investigators consistently prioritised their careers over their romantic relationships. If only she could be so single-minded and absorbed in her job. She had a pile of corrections awaiting her that would ordinarily have been marked by now.

Jane had never felt particularly passionate about teaching, not even in the early days. Nowadays, so much of her time was taken up with lesson planning, department meetings, and identifying teaching objectives that her teaching had suffered. Any spontaneity or creative spirit that might once have been a defining characteristic of her lessons had been squashed by the need to conform with the department's objectives and the new principal's obsession with paper trails.

Having always found the romantic portrayals of female English teachers in literature and on screen to be compelling, she had thought that teaching for a few years would be a satisfying stopgap on her way to literary success. It was a dream she did not openly discuss with her family. Her father was not much of a reader, and her mother was fond of formulaic romances with cookie-cutter characters and predictable storylines.

When Jane had announced that she would like one day to be a published author, her mother had crinkled her nose in a mixture of disapproval and disgust. At the time, she took her mother's obvious irritation as evidence that the idea was fanciful and better left alone. In retrospect, having seen that same expression whenever her father had mentioned local politics or regional weather warnings, she wondered if it had indicated mere disinterest.

Jane knew she could ignore the outside world for only so long. Her mother was the type of person who would drive halfway across the country if either daughter left her calls unreturned for more than a few days. Jane had never viewed this behaviour as evidence of maternal love, but rather, as a reflection of her mother's inability and unwillingness to let others be.

Meanwhile, Charlotte seemed to be floating on air. Having shared her baby news with their parents, who were over the moon, she was now flooding Jane with baby names and links to articles about pregnancy, as if Jane herself were with child. It was only a matter of time before her self-obsessed sister attempted a welfare check. The thought would never occur to Charlotte that her sister might not care to hear about the minutiae of every bout of morning sickness.

When eleven days had elapsed since her date with John, Jane picked up the phone and called her mother, and then Charlotte. She listened to what they had to say, which was plenty, and apologised profusely for not having responded more fully to their messages and updates. Didn't Jane understand that a thumbs-up was passive aggressive, and a heart emoji dismissive? No, she didn't. Or, maybe she did, but her intentions had not been to hurt or offend. She did not explain that choosing the most appropriate emoji for a text message ranked very low on her list of priorities. She did not convey her devastating disappointment to either of them, nor did she make any reference to John.

On the nights when sleep eluded her, she often succumbed to bouts of paranoia. She imagined he was talking about her behind her back with his friends. She pictured them all laughing, seated at a round, wooden table in McDaid's, a fashionable pub on the outskirts of Glin, where people like John drank with their childhood friends when they came back from college. In the cold light of morning, she realised that she was insignificant in his eyes, and that felt worse than being the object of his ridicule and scorn.

She picked up her phone and dialled Sara's number. Seven years ago, she had attended Sara's wedding with Daniel. It was the last social occasion they attended as a couple before he announced he was leaving her. In retrospect, she realised he had been less than enthusiastic on that day, and, particularly, on that night. She presumed his apathy stemmed from the fact that he knew fewer people at the event than she did, but he had been a close friend of Sara's brother for years by that stage and was probably better acquainted with the family than she was. Apart from the occasional text wishing each other a merry Christmas or a happy birthday, neither Jane nor Sara would classify the other as a close friend any longer.

Circumstances had thrown them together in college. They shared a mutual friend and a few tutorials in common, as well as a healthy disdain for International Commerce students. Sara was softly spoken, but people, including most of the lecturers, hung on her every word. It may have been her habit of pausing just before delivering the last few words of each sentence that hooked their attention. Sara was the only daughter of two university lecturers who had always lavished her with praise and listened to her as if she were their equal. She expected others to listen, even if she was waffling on about something she didn't fully grasp. Didn't Jane's mother always say that you get what you expect from other people?

People often asked if Jane and Sara were sisters, despite one being a tall, broad-shouldered redhead, and the other a delicate, elfin blonde. They both possessed a dreamy quality and were always seemingly lost in thought and frequently late for class but were brilliant and ambitious students with exacting minds. For two such academically driven friends, they had never cared to compete with each other or with anyone else. Their minds were firmly fixed on attaining a first in their final exams, and if one placed slightly higher than the other in the class ranking, then so be it.

The phone rang until it went to voicemail. When it was time to leave a message, Jane chickened out. It hadn't been a good idea to call in the first place. They hadn't chatted by phone in years. She might not have received an invitation to Sara's wedding had she not been married to her younger brother's best friend. Sara had two young boys now, but their names eluded Jane. Her phone buzzed.

Call you back in a while. Busy with the kids, Sara's message read.

Jane suspected it was a standard message that automatically went out to anyone whose call Sara missed. She was not too hopeful about the prospect of a return call. She would come across as completely self-absorbed anyway, calling with the sole purpose of talking about a relationship problem, after such a long hiatus in contact. She started to scroll back through their message thread to find the children's names. There it was, Senan, the second boy. Eighteen months earlier, Eoin. Suddenly the phone vibrated in her hand. Now that the moment had arrived, she was overtaken by a queasy feeling; a sign urging her not to betray herself. But she swallowed her pride and steeled herself for the conversation that lay ahead.

"Hello, hello!" Jane turned up the charm, infusing warmth and humour into her voice. She felt it would be insincere to make small talk, and to pretend to be calling for a long over-due catch-up. She'd have to keep things upbeat, but she wasn't here to rebuild old bridges. She wanted the opinion of a trusted acquaintance who knew both her and John, and whose opinion she respected.

"So good to hear from you, Jane!" Sara sounded tired.

"Is it an OK time for you? You're not busy with Senan and Eoin?" She was glad she'd had the time to retrieve their names.

"Oh, no, they're in bed ages. I'm just sitting here with my feet up waiting for Gordon. It was such a lovely surprise to see your name pop up on my phone. You won't believe it, but I was thinking about you only last week."

Jane could never understand why people considered it a compliment to tell someone they'd thought about them recently. She thought about a lot of people, and many of them were not particularly memorable or likeable. Minds were like that. They pulled the strangest of memories from the depths of one's consciousness for reasons she'd never understand.

"How's Gordon?" Jane asked, trying to sound enthusiastic about a man to whom she had never warmed.

Gordon was a consultant who earned great money and was a highly respected member of the community, but he had a huge personality deficit and mediocre looks. Sara could have been a model, were it not for her short stature. In fact, she was too conventionally pretty to make it as a model. She outshone her husband in every sense.

"Oh, great," Sara said. "He's in Beaumont now. Working in respiratory health."

"That's amazing, Sara!" Jane exclaimed.

Hadn't his father been a hospital doctor, too? Wasn't it always easier to secure those positions if you were well connected? Sara gave a full report on both her sons before turning the spotlight on Jane. "How's everything going with you?"

"Well, Sara, I guess that's why I'm calling. You have always been so wise."

"Me, wise?" Her old friend's delight was palpable, "I'm not so sure about that."

It was the truth. There were half a dozen people with whom Jane could have chatted about her current situation. But she didn't want to consult a yes-woman who would encourage her to harbour wild and unrealistic fantasies; she wanted the opinion of someone she respected, who would speak frankly and not spare her feelings, with some insight into John's character.

"OK, long story short. Do you remember that thing I had with John Davy?"

"Yes!" Sara replied. "Of course. We couldn't believe it. You two snogged, right?"

Jane hated that word. It brought the image of a warthog to mind. There was nothing remotely romantic about it. Plus, she and John had never actually kissed, but only shared a moment that Jane had obsessed over for months afterwards. "As you know, nothing came of it."

"He never called you back, I remember. You won't have been the only girl!" Sara's tone was consolatory.

"Well, he got back in touch, and we met up recently. And he told me all these things about me being the one, and—"

"Slow down, Jane. I'm aghast." There was no trace of shock in her voice, however.

"He never called after that. That was nearly two weeks ago – eleven days, to be exact. What do you think? You kind of know him, don't you?" Jane cringed at how desperate she must sound.

"Well, all I know about John Davy is that he recently split with his wife, who's impossibly good-looking, really smart, and has a brilliant job in a corporate law firm."

"Oh God, so I'm wasting my time." John Davy was on the rebound. He was using her for an ego boost, and nothing more. He had shown no interest in sleeping with her, preferring to return alone to his hotel room at the not so ungodly hour of midnight.

"Hold on, I didn't say that. I mean, just because things didn't work out with what's-her-face. Stockbrokers work crazy hours, and she was a workaholic, too."

Jane sensed an air of condescension in her friend's tone, as if she thought Jane wouldn't understand the harsh reality of working in the private sector. At one time in her life, Sara would have looked down on the job of a solicitor; now, she seemed to delight in being part of the corporate elite that she had openly mocked in college. "But, as you said, he has a track record of not calling girls back."

"I didn't say that. It's just, he was so popular, and there were so many girls who followed him around. He had no choice but to blank some of them. Not that you stalked him, but you know, he was so popular."

"And that's not what I want, if I'm honest. We're not in the same league."

"Oh, Jane, that was back then. Weren't we all desperate in college? I chased that awful guy from Social Science around for two years, just because he looked like Boris Becker. He had no interest in me, but maybe that was the attraction."

Jane laughed, remembering why she had found Sara so amusing, and feeling a sharp pang of regret at not having stayed in touch. But they had drifted apart for a reason.

"Boris Becker! That's a blast from the past. You were far too good for him, anyway. He wore black lace-ups with his jeans, remember?" Jane had thought that Gordon was a step down from Boris, despite having reassured Sara at the time that he was a catch and a keeper.

"Look, I bet you'll hear back from him in a few days," Sara said, unconvincingly. "I'm going to ask around to try to find out if there's anyone else on the scene. If there's anything to find out, Caroline will know about it."

Jane cast about in her memory for Carolines.

"Gordon's sister," Sara added.

"Oh, she knows John?" Jane was surprised. Caroline had been the dour bridesmaid who had insisted on doing the Prayer of the Faithful, robbing Sara's dowager aunt of her one and only role in the wedding ceremony.

"Yes, and they're very close."

"Really? They don't seem like they'd be friends."

"Well, they are." Sara sounded affronted. "They studied together, and they know lots of the same people."

"Oh! Great! Well, if you think you can trust her not to run back with stories to John—"

"Of course. Caroline is the soul of discretion," Sara said reassuringly.

How things had changed in a few short years! Sara had suspected Caroline of trying to sabotage her hen night by talking incessantly of her own failed marriage and how everyone in the Mallon family was doomed to unhappiness.

"I'm sure she's very discreet, but if she's a friend of his, she's not going to have anything negative to say about him."

Sara laughed knowingly. "That's where you're wrong. Caroline is a very straight talker."

"Well, I'd be so grateful if you could enquire."

"Shall we meet for lunch, then? After I confer with Caroline?"

Jane would have preferred to receive the information over the phone. She knew it was selfish of her to contact Sara out of the blue and to expect Sara to do her bidding. "Lovely. Let me know when suits! You're busy. I can come anytime." Jane would meet her for lunch and pay for it and admire Sara's photos of her offspring. It was the least she could do.

"OK. Sit tight. I'll get my detective hat on!"

"Thank you, Sara. You're a star." Jane ached to ask the question that no self-respecting woman would. If John Davy were out of her league, her oldest college friend would be the one to tell her. It would have been a relief to hear that John was out of her league and had been hard work even for the impossibly beautiful corporate lawyer.

After hanging up, she leaned back, and an unexpected arch of sunlight adorned the foot of her bed. There was a lot to be said for resigning oneself to one's fate. Perhaps Sara would return with the news that John was seeing numerous women. That, having had his heart shattered, he was acting out in the strangest of ways. Jane could then return to her normal life, disillusioned and hopeless. Once again, she would be able to enjoy the company of her friends without the constant compulsion to check her phone. She drifted into a deep and restorative sleep, only to be woken by the loud double beep of her phone.

It was a text message from John.

CHAPTER FOURTEEN
The Invitation

Hi Jane, hope you're well! I've been run ragged at work these last two weeks but have thought about you often. I'll be in Dublin next month, but maybe you'd like to visit me in London before then?

She read John's message a few times over to make sure she wasn't imagining things. He had thought of her over the last two weeks. He was inviting her to come and see him in London! Her heart skipped a beat. She decided not to respond immediately. He had waited eleven days to follow up from their date, so she would make him wait at least two hours for her answer. She shoved her phone under the pillow and removed herself from the bedroom. She had an hour before Charlotte and Neil were due to come over. She decided to go for a walk.

Outside, the air was fresh and breezy. The movement and sunlight were invigorating, and her indignation gradually gave way to pragmatism. They didn't know each other. He owed her nothing. They were moving slowly, as they should, especially as he had only just come out of a marriage.

She couldn't quite get her head around the fact that she would be flying to London in the coming weeks to visit John Davy. Was he her boyfriend? They had yet to define the relationship, but this was where they were headed. Christmas was a few weeks away. Might she be brought up to the family home and introduced to his parents? She had met them before, but back then she was an employee, not a future daughter-in-law.

It was the natural next step, especially in your thirties. Hadn't Charlotte often noted how quickly relationships progress when you're older and you know your own mind? Well, Jane knew her own mind. And John had obviously gotten very clear on the type of future he wanted. She wondered if she shouldn't play a little harder to get. Upon further reflection, she decided against it. She wanted John to desire her presence and long for her company because of who she was, not because of the games she was playing. She was so caught up in her thoughts as she rounded the corner onto Mill Lane that she collided with a workman in muddy, industrial-looking boots and a luminous yellow coat.

"Hello, Jane!" came a voice from under his white hardhat.

The wind whipped Jane's hair back into her eyes as she tried to discern the identity of the labourer.

"I can see I've caught you off-guard." He tipped back his hat to reveal his face, a smile breaking effortlessly across it.

"William! I'm so sorry I didn't recognise you at first." She tucked a wisp of stray hair behind her ear. How dishevelled she must look compared to the last time they'd met.

"No problem. Well, watch out. It's set to get very windy later."

The profound happiness she had been feeling suddenly deserted her. Had she misgauged his interest during their previous encounters? Or was he feigning this breezy indifference to save face? These thoughts ricocheted inside her head as she fumbled for the front door key.

How ridiculous that her ego was tormenting her on what should be the happiest day of her life. Reminding herself that she had no interest in William, she busied herself for the next hour with frying mince for the shepherd's pie. Although she tried to keep her mind on the task at hand, she began to fantasise about John's life. She imagined that his friendship group was composed entirely of sophisticated, confident couples, who endlessly speculated about the mysterious woman who had wrought such changes in their friend.

The short, sharp ring of the doorbell trespassed on her daydream. Could it be William, having spotted which house was hers? She cringed at her own neediness. As soon as a man lost interest in Jane, she wanted to win it back. Margaret had exaggerated how good-looking he was. He had approached them in the pub that night but had nothing funny or amusing to say for himself. John would have made some witty comment and offered to buy them a drink. Suddenly irked at William's oversight, she pulled back the curtain to reveal Charlotte's anxious face. She was early and on her own.

"Hi! Where's Neil?" Jane said, immediately clocking, from Charlotte's sheepish expression, that this was not the right question to ask.

Charlotte breezed past and dropped her shopping bags in the hall. "Men!" Charlotte hissed. "They're bloody useless."

Jane followed her sister into the sitting room. The thought of John's message awaiting her response gave her sustenance. Charlotte lowered herself onto the sofa with what Jane considered to be unnecessary care. Her laboured breathing and pained expression gave the impression of being under duress, but her bump was still barely visible, and she was still wearing the tiny, navy-blue kimono she'd worn on Christmas Day last year.

This was the first time Jane had seen her sister really angry with Neil. "Well, can I help you out?" Jane dreaded the thought of assembling an Ikea cot with her sister, but she felt assured that her offer would never be taken up.

"Not unless you have something in your medicine cabinet that will change his personality."

"I do have a very sharp nail scissors and some headlice spray."

"That would be too good for him, Jane. He's been an utter prick since I told him I was pregnant."

"I thought he was delighted. I mean, he seemed so chuffed." Jane cast her memory back to the day in the restaurant. Hadn't he been almost charming?

"I thought so, too, until he started outlining all the ways in which his life would not change after the baby's born."

Jane carefully chose her words, not wanting any criticism she might make of Neil thrown back in her face when the couple patched up their differences in the near future. Wanting an early night, she had hoped Charlotte's visit would be a brief and amicable one, but as the evening wore on, and Charlotte forgot about whatever it was that Neil had or hadn't done, the two sisters chatted easily.

Jane wondered if Neil's dark and brooding presence had been the reason they'd grown apart in recent years. Now that her sister was pregnant with his child, Neil Tully would be a permanent presence in all their lives. Their parents seemed to like him. He ticked all the boxes, as far as their mother was concerned. He had been educated in the right schools, and his parents were presentable and reasonably wealthy. Claire was willing to overlook his middling academic career, as he had made a huge success of the family business, and that took its own type of intelligence. Neil was hardworking and driven; their father could relate to that. And Charlotte adored him, much to the confoundment of her elder sister.

Charlotte's phone beeped intermittently over the course of the evening, and she studiously ignored it. At around ten, they heard a gentle knocking at the front door. Jane jumped; Charlotte seemed less surprised. Within a matter of minutes, Neil had recited a condescending apology and was gently guiding Charlotte out to his car, with his hand on her lower back. *Thank you*, he mouthed over his shoulder to Jane.

Jane smiled weakly, feeling compromised. She could clearly see how the balance of power had tipped once again in Neil's favour. She thought of her parents. At times, Claire bemoaned her husband's uncommunicativeness. Jane was certain that her mother's emotional needs were seldom, if ever, met, but her father was not a manipulative person.

Jane went upstairs, pulled her phone from under the pillow, and set about composing a message that would convey insouciance and humour in equal measure. After several false starts, she repaired to her sitting room where she hoped to find inspiration in a glass of red wine. Tucked up under one of the numerous plush pink blankets that lay in various locations around her freezing home, she waited for the warm, fuzzy feeling to kick in. Before she knew it, the sentences were flowing.

She had always been enamoured with the idea of a man who would love her in her rawest form. Someone with whom she could be herself without fearing rejection. Didn't all the books on self-esteem say the same thing? Hadn't her therapist, Jacq, always warned her about changing herself to please others? It made complete sense. This man had been in her life since childhood. He knew what he was getting into when he contacted her out of the blue.

Jane read over the text she had crafted. It was effusive, but a real man, with serious intentions, would not be turned off. Before she could second-guess herself, she pressed the send button, and then she poured herself a third glass of wine.

CHAPTER FIFTEEN
The Eyes of the Beholder

The blasts of a car horn coming in through the bedroom window alerted Jane that Margaret had pulled up outside. If it hadn't been so cold, Margaret would have come to the door and knocked. Jane always had her phone switched off or on silent these days. Jane threw on her violet woolly cardigan, checked that her hair was pinned correctly at the back, and picked up the satchel she had carefully packed the night before.

Jane had been correcting examination papers in bed all weekend. She had taken to doing everything in bed of late. Upon arriving home, she would change into pyjamas and bed socks and tuck herself neatly into her queen-sized bed. The last few days had been filled with reading, correcting, and watching TV. The message she had drunkenly sent to John on Wednesday, suggesting she fly out to spend that very weekend with him, had been left unanswered. She suspected that he had been turned off by her honesty.

She had no idea what was going on with him. Was he this inconsistent in other areas of his life as well? Surely, he could not have achieved his current level of career success by flitting from one idea to the next, as his enthusiasm waxed and waned. She cast her mind back to his friendships. Was he still friends with the people he had been close to in his college years? She couldn't really say for certain. To the best of her knowledge, the private school set tended to stick together throughout their higher education.

Her mind was constantly elsewhere, thinking about what he might be doing at various points of the day. Although she presumed otherwise, she hoped that she crossed his mind occasionally. Almost two months on from his original message, they had met once, sort of kissed (if a peck on the lips counted), held hands, and communicated sporadically by text. A pattern seemed to be emerging. She braced herself for the agony of waiting. Sooner or later, John Davy would reappear in her inbox and move things to the next level, but only at his pace.

Given her uptight demeanour when Margaret had enquired about the trip to London, Margaret had since tried to keep to neutral topics of conversation. Jane was happy to listen to her best friend's dealings with builders and a stroppy architect.

"I just can't handle any more of his tantrums," Margaret declared.

"Can't you get rid of him? There must be plenty of other architects out there," Jane said, visualising herself and John Davy jetting off somewhere exotic. He would have his hand on the small of her back as she looked for something in her hand luggage. A look of concerned calm would suffuse his features as the other passengers looked on, in envy, at the extremely attractive couple.

"I'm talking about Frank!" Margaret looked across at Jane's bewildered face.

"Frank?"

"I don't know, he's been acting weird. It's almost as if something clicked when we signed the contract. Maybe he realised that this is it, and he's stuck with me for life."

"Well, not necessarily." Jane turned to look at Margaret's profile. Her cheekbones were more prominent than usual. "I mean, you're not tied to him forever. Houses can be sold."

"You're not getting it. I don't want to sell the house. I just want Frank back to being his usual self and being happy with me and his life."

"He's not unhappy. It's probably just stress, you know."

Margaret unclenched her jaw, the softness returning to her face. "Do you think so?"

"Definitely! And Frank is a perfectionist, you know that. He won't rest till everything is in order."

"You're right. It'll be fine, it's just the stress of having builders living on top of us."

Jane sensed an uneasiness in her friend's tone, as if she regretted having aired her dirty laundry. Margaret was always fiercely private; willing to lend a listening ear and dispense sage advice when called upon, but never one to bare her soul. Margaret turned on the radio, twisting the knob to raise the volume.

She was an avid news fan, and Jane had often overheard her in the staff room, talking on the phone to her mother about an item from the morning bulletin. Everyone else would be talking about their plans for the weekend, and Margaret would be on a call to someone at home, asking what they thought of some politician's inappropriate comment in the Dáil chamber. Jane wasn't sure if Frank had any real knowledge of politics. He was certainly smart, and had a first in Engineering from Trinity, but she wasn't sure if she'd call him intelligent. He could have been, if he read outside of his field.

Margaret reversed badly into the one remaining staff parking space outside the school's main entrance, and the two women switched into teacher mode, leaving their personal lives very much behind. Two Sixth Year girls pulled up alongside in a car that was newer, shinier and more expensive than any of the teachers' vehicles. They waved as they emerged from its doors, without as much as a copybook in sight. Margaret dramatically rolled her eyes, and Jane felt heartened by the reappearance of her old friend's good humour.

"Morning, girls!" she chirped, before turning to Jane. "Where in the hell do they think they're going today?"

"Knowing Harriet, the cinema!"

The day dragged on. How was it that some days were so much more boring than others? Jane knocked back the tar-like coffee before leaving the staffroom for her afternoon classes. The students mirrored their teacher's apathy back to her. Jane usually could trace back even the minutest change in her mood to a fleeting thought from hours earlier. When had her day taken a turn for the worse? Was it the idle chat at break time about wedding outfits? The thought that she might have to attend Charlotte and Neil's garish ceremony without a plus-one did nothing to buoy her spirits.

Burying her phone under a pile of copies in her desk drawer for four consecutive afternoon classes had only increased her anticipation of a message from John. When she finally managed to usher out the stragglers from her final class, she was fit to burst with excitement. It had been two days since she'd made the ridiculous suggestion that she fly out to meet him. She closed her eyes for a moment, willing there to be a message. When she fished her phone from the bottom of the drawer and saw the empty screen, her heart dropped.

Nothing! Unbelievable. What an absolute piece of crap John Davy was! What a cheeky, entitled way to conduct oneself with someone he'd known all his life? The anger coursing through her veins was enlivening, mobilising even. She walked down the stairs and through multiple corridors to the main hall with a newfound sense of purpose. She was going to show that middle-aged ponce, who was dramatically overestimating his appeal, not to mess with her. She was no longer the clumsy, unattractive class swot. She had blossomed, and she knew her worth. Who was he to presume that a bone thrown her way, every once in a while, would suffice to keep her interest?

She walked out of the main doors and approached Margaret's car.

"Hello, hello!" Margaret greeted Jane in her usual upbeat manner. "Hop in!"

Jane could only presume that she was no longer fretting about Frank. "Feeling better?" she enquired tentatively, belting herself into the passenger seat and placing her backpack on the floor by her feet.

"About what?" Margaret's breezy attitude surprised Jane.

"The house?" Jane didn't want to remind her that Frank had been the source of her annoyance.

"Oh, that," Margaret said. "I've moved past it now. While my Second Years were writing their essays, I happened to recall the time Frank met me off the Cork train in Euston Station in the early days of our courtship with a bouquet of red roses."

"He did that?" Jane found it difficult to picture Frank making such an extravagant gesture.

"And this led me to remember that on our first Christmas together, he gave me a card he had made himself. He had drawn the two of us in side profile, looking out at the sea."

Jane couldn't disguise her astonishment. "I didn't even know the man could draw!"

"He's quite talented. You know what was hilarious, he made himself taller – a head and shoulders above me. And he made me look all pretty and delicate. Me, Jane!"

"You are incredibly pretty! What are you talking about?"

"I'm invisible. Men never look twice at me. But in the drawing, I saw the way I looked through his eyes."

Jane had to admit that perhaps Frank was not simply dead weight, as she had thought. Anyway, who was she to judge him? He had been Margaret's college boyfriend, and he had remained true for all these years.

"Okey-dokey," Margaret said as they pulled up opposite Jane's cottage.

It had been a ten-minute journey, but for Jane, it had felt like a lifetime. She hoisted her backpack onto one shoulder and gently closed the door. "Bye, Margaret! Thank you!"

She watched her friend drive away, toward the beautiful new home she shared with Frank, the only man she'd ever loved. How lucky Margaret was to have a man who would choose her. And here she was, chasing after some man who was out of her league and clearly not interested. She sighed and walked up the path to her cottage.

CHAPTER SIXTEEN
REUNION

When Jane walked into the modern European restaurant, she was surprised to find Sara and her elder son sitting at a table strewn with dirty plates, napkins, and empty bottles of mineral water. Her younger son was dozing in his stroller. Having been there for well over an hour without notifying Jane of any change of plan, Sara had already ordered and consumed her meal. Having kids meant you could do things like that without seeming rude, Jane reckoned. Jane went over and gave Sara a hug before sitting in the only chair that was not already occupied by a diaper bag and other toddler-related accessories.

Jane had not had much experience with children, as she and Charlotte were very short on cousins. On her mother's side, there was one cousin: a strange, furtive child, who had grown into a strange, furtive adult. Eimear wouldn't acknowledge her if they passed on the street. Her father's brothers, both of whom had remained bachelors, had taken over the family farm in Glin when their father had died.

Jane enjoyed the company of children when she could have an intelligent conversation with them, even if it was only about killer worms or Arthur Conan Doyle's falling out with Harry Houdini. Her neighbour on Mill Lane had two boys who occasionally stood at the low wall that separated their gardens. They reminded her of old men.

The last time the elder boy had spied her taking clothes in from the washing line, he had swooped in with one of his deadly questions. Would she rather wrestle with an alligator whose stomach was full or run from an escaped lion who hadn't eaten in days?

Infants, who gurgled with their heads lolling around or screamed incessantly like wounded cats, held no attraction for her. Toddlers, who wore frenzied looks and defied their parents' requests to put something down or eat a fish finger, terrified her. She wondered if many parents regretted having had children.

The chubby toddler sitting opposite her now with peas smeared on his cheeks, opening his mouth periodically to reveal a mouthful of chewed carrot, was far from charming. How was it that very good-looking women had such ordinary-looking children? This was his first time meeting Jane, and he must have sensed she had no interest in how his day had been at preschool or what his favourite cartoon was. She asked anyway, and he responded with a snarl.

Sara seemed not to notice his churlishness. Most parents seemed to be oblivious to how obnoxious their offspring were. Perhaps she even found him endearing. Later that night, she might relay the details of this child's rudeness to his father, who would probably chortle as if it were the funniest thing he'd ever heard. Her own mother, Claire, had always said that children were little adults, and that nastiness in a child was no different from that in an adult. This little guy, Jane thought, would surely grow up to be as arrogant as his father.

Sara's face looked drawn, and the shadows under her eyes were more pronounced than Jane remembered. Being so incredibly thin couldn't have helped. She was five foot three and about a hundred pounds. Senan stayed peacefully asleep. Eoin's attention was focussed on his mother's phone, the latest offering from Samsung. Jane had heard that the cameras were good, which was especially useful if you were documenting your children's lives on an hourly basis.

When had her bookish friend become so slick? At university, Sara's charm had lain in her insouciance: honey-blonde curls tied in a loose knot atop her head, a barely visible sweep of mascara on her fair lashes. The colourful runners were her only concession to the world of fashion. She wore high-waisted, flared jeans; simple long-sleeved tops in nautical stripes; and no jewellery except for pearl earrings.

Nowadays, she never left the house without perfectly applied winged eyeliner, straightened hair with an impossibly blunt fringe, drop earrings, and a brightly coloured designer dress. The formerly square-cut, fiercely practical nails were a different colour every week, or so Jane had heard from the other girls in their friendship group, whose observations spoke to envy rather than disapproval.

Jane felt refreshingly unfinished next to the varnished version of her old college chum. She watched as the immaculately presented mother reproved the elder of the two boys for not finishing his carrots, picking up the spoon to finish the task herself. It had surprised Jane that the daughter of two such bright and cultured academics could be so impressed by a man's medical degree. Sara's father had written books on Irish politics, and her mother was a lecturer in the archaeology department of UCD. Their tumbledown cottage in Sandymount had character and charm in spades. But Sara had left that life behind her.

Everyone raved about how well she looked these days, but Jane couldn't help thinking that Sara had sold her natural beauty for a bland symmetry that made her appear almost identical to every other woman with the money to fix what nature hadn't provided. No longer an ethereal beauty, she had become yet another participant in the beauty rat race, with minimal amounts of filler carefully injected into certain points on her face, including her lower lip.

"Reading anything interesting at the moment?" Jane enquired, hoping that somewhere beneath the polished exterior lay the girl who would skip lunch to read Thomas Hardy in the best seat in the library, the corner one next to the radiator, beside the double window.

"Nothing at the moment."

"You're too busy with the kids. In a few years—"

"Maybe." Sara seemed disinterested. "So much drama in our lives with these two, neither of us get to do much in the way of hobbies these days."

"Well, I just finished *Middlemarch*. God, it was hard going—"

"Oh, I read that years ago. It really was a depressing read. I mainly listen to crime podcasts now. Speaking of which, I have been doing some investigative work of my own."

Jane's cheeks flushed. "Oh God."

"So, Caroline is friends with both him and his ex-wife, which I hadn't known."

Jane shuddered at the thought of an ex-wife, especially one who would have Caroline as a friend. "You didn't mention me, did you? It'll get back to him."

"Of course I didn't! Caroline would definitely tell the ex-wife everything. They're very close."

"Oh, thank God for that. So, do you know why they split?" Jane's eyes widened in anticipation. She averted her gaze, in case Sara's expression betrayed something dreadful.

A meek-looking waitress arrived with a menu for Jane. As she recited the day's specials, Sara cut her off with a request for Eoin's dinner to be reheated. Since when had Sara become so brash? Had there been signs of this rudeness back in their college days? Perhaps Jane had overlooked them because they didn't fit with her perception of Sara.

Jane ordered the soup of the day, which was potato and leek, followed by a chicken Caesar salad and a lemon drop martini. When Sara excused herself to go and change Senan, Jane found herself seated opposite a disgruntled toddler who refused to make eye contact. She pretended to be in conversation with him. When Sara eventually returned with a chirpy looking infant, Jane's soup had still not arrived. Now that Senan was fed, and his nappy had been changed, he was eager to engage with Jane. He sat on his mother's lap, entranced and following Jane's every gesture with a level of interest she had never experienced before. She almost felt under pressure to perform. Sara took a long sip of her sparkling water before nodding knowingly in the direction of Jane's cocktail glass.

"Gone are those days for me!" She looked off into the distance, as if recalling happier times. "Well, Caroline said that their relationship was not strong enough to sustain children. His ex-wife, Liz, is very career driven and they argued non-stop about who was doing what. Just the usual parenthood squabbles."

"So they're not getting back together, then?" Jane was wondering if the relationship had not been very strong in the first place.

"No, definitely not! They're on the road to divorce. But, you know, there were times when I felt like walking out on Gordon. The arguments we had about whose turn it was for a lie-in!"

"What's your feeling, Sara? Is he someone that would make a good partner?" Jane hated that word, but at thirty-seven, she felt a little ridiculous referring to a man as her boyfriend.

"Well, not for Liz. She's nothing like you, though."

Stung by Sara's words, Jane was afraid to ask her for clarification. Liz clearly was someone who didn't put up with nonsense. She had ended the relationship and turfed John out when she realised that he wasn't willing to pull his weight. Jane, on the other hand, would suffer in silence and hope against hope that he'd learn to share the burden of parenthood. She knew she was a walk-over – the long-suffering, hopeful type of person who gave people, and especially men, every last chance to prove themselves. She was the embodiment of female desperation. She'd have hung in till the bitter end, never for a moment imagining that there might be someone better than John Davy out there for her.

"Liz was the one who wanted to split up, then?" Jane wondered what it would be like to sit across the table from her.

"Oh, yes. But that's not to say he isn't glad to be out of it. They fought like cats and dogs, apparently."

Jane's starter and main course arrived at the same time, which suited her fine as she was starving.

"Didn't Caroline wonder why you were so curious about his marriage?" Jane refilled her glass from the jug of tap water Sara had ordered for the children. The last thing she needed was to get tipsy over lunch and for the news to filter back to John that she'd turned to alcohol in her middle age.

"No, I just told her that I saw Dee recently, so I was curious how things had worked out for him. You know, Dee married his friend and former colleague, the third partner in the firm. James O'Halloran is the other guy. You remember him?"

"Yeah, I think so," Jane conceded, afraid to admit the full extent of her snooping. She had perused photos of James's wedding, his wife's thirtieth, and their children's various birthday parties over the last few weeks on Facebook, in hopes of catching sight of John in the background.

"Well, the guy that Dee married has left the firm. Some really ordinary guy, not particularly good-looking, quite chubby, really. Went to school with your John."

Jane had almost forgotten about Denise O'Callaghan, John's beautiful on/off college girlfriend. She had heard rumours that Dee had gone off with his work colleague and friend a few years later. The fact that they had all stayed friends struck her as incredibly mature.

"I knew they were together in college, and again, later, for a while, but I always thought he and Dee were more friends than anything else."

Jane had never felt threatened by Dee, despite her being gorgeous, clever, and annoyingly popular. She was almost too gorgeous to be a threat. The fact that Sara and Jane knew so much about her, without her being even aware of their existence, was testament to her cult status. Everyone wanted to be like Dee O'Callaghan. And since no one could really measure up they all tried to be friends with her, or, at the very least, to be seen in her circle.

"Looks like John's not as much of a catch as we all thought he was! But, not to rain on your parade." Sara bit her lip.

"Why? What's he done, Sara?" Jane buried her face in her hands.

"Oh, nothing, really. He's just not a very good husband. Well, that's not fair – he just wasn't a very good husband to Liz. He's a workaholic. And, I guess, so is she. They fought over who did what, and he called her some awful names."

"I take it that Caroline took Liz's side?"

"Not really. She just said that they brought out the worst in each other. But, as I said, you are nothing like Liz. You two could work really well together."

"Do you really think so?" Jane couldn't help feeling that Sara was backtracking somewhat. "When you said he's not much of a catch, did you really mean that?"

Sara looked right at her this time and said, in almost too measured a manner, "No, he's still a catch, but he's not perfect. None of us is."

Strangely reassured by Sara's qualification of her earlier remark, Jane felt a spark of hope. *None of us is perfect.* It wasn't as if Jane had an uncheckered past. She'd had a failed marriage, a handful of very short-lived relationships that were prematurely ended by the men in question, and a few unfortunate misreads on her part. The kindly bursar in St Mary's, who took her under his wing after her divorce, had been interested in a young, pretty Geography trainee teacher named Mark.

Then, when she attended a group tennis lesson several years ago, she'd had her eye on a decidedly plain but very cerebral barrister for the duration of the term. When he suggested they all go for a drink with the coach on the twelfth and final night of term, she had been certain that he'd make his move. But it became evident from early in the evening that he only had eyes for the rugged Australian coach, who was straight but glad of the compliment. In the aftermath of her split with Daniel, these misunderstandings served only to strengthen her belief that she lacked the ability to read the room, as it were.

Jane inserted her card into the machine and absentmindedly punched in her pin number. After she had hugged Sara goodbye, smiled sweetly at Eoin, and patted Senan on the head, she walked towards her bus stop. The glimmer of hope was snuffed out when she caught a sidelong glimpse of herself in a bookshop window. With her unkempt hair and rounded shoulders, how had she ever thought that someone like John Davy could find her attractive? His ex-girlfriends were all so polished and well-presented. Sara must think her equal parts fantasist and fool.

She imagined the conversation Sara would have with Gordon later that day. Jane suspected that Gordon liked her the least out of all his wife's friends, as she was completely unimpressed by his achievements and was visibly uncomfortable in his presence. The more she tried to forge a connection with him, the greater her sense of unease. When she arrived at the bus stop, she had no desire to wait there passively. Anger bubbled up inside her and she had a strong desire to keep moving. But the grey clouds looming overhead looked ominous, and she had a light jacket and no umbrella.

She launched into a daydream about all the ways she would humiliate John. She trawled through her memory for men who had passed her up for someone else. There had been plenty. She imagined a future in which she had achieved huge literary success and would pass these men in the street while looking magnificent and smiling blankly at them, as if embarrassed by her inability to recall their names.

John would read about her in the paper, hear about her from his mother, and regret losing out on his chance with a successful author, an unconventional beauty, a quirky yet sophisticated woman who was different from his usual type. She would be gracious and forgiving, mainly because she had moved on, but also because it would make the men feel irrelevant. In this fantasy life, she no longer needed a man. As the bus arrived, her phone vibrated against her hipbone. She reached for her wallet, glimpsing a message on her phone from – of course, John Davy.

Wasn't life ironic? Just when she'd given up on him, he reached out. It was as if, in some way, they were connected, and he could sense her pulling away. Now that the message had arrived, now that he had done what she had been willing him to do for the past three days, she felt no urgency to read it. It wasn't that she was uninterested – she was dying to see what he'd written, and whether he'd suggest she visit the following weekend instead – but as long as she didn't read the message, she couldn't be disappointed. And for now, she was happy to sit with the hope that he was willing to take things to the next stage. She would wait until the following morning to read his message. She would enjoy making him squirm.

CHAPTER SEVENTEEN
Chance Encounter

Three days later, Jane found herself in the departure lounge of Dublin airport, sitting on her hands and waiting for a very early morning flight to London City Airport. The morning after receiving John's long-awaited text, she had opened it to find that it comprised one sentence.

Are you free to travel to London this coming Friday?

She knew that clearing her schedule at such short notice smacked of desperation. And yet, she had acquiesced. The day in question fell six days before Christmas and coincided with the last day of house exams at St Mary's. As all the English and Irish exams would be over by then, she would not be needed on that day. She had an early morning exam hall supervision for a First Year Religion exam but could easily find someone to stand in for her.

Her mind had been in overdrive ever since. She tormented herself with all the aspects of John and his life that were less than satisfactory. Was it strange that he had a child to whom he rarely made even oblique references in his text messages? It was one thing to omit to mention the ex-wife, as she was history, an excisable part of one's past.

On the flight, she closed her eyes and inhaled deeply several times to calm her nerves. The cold rush from the air conditioning vent above her head had already dried out her sinuses. This was supposed to be an epoch in her existence, travelling to be with the only man who'd ever lived up to her romantic ideal, and yet she was fit to strangle her neighbouring passenger, an American woman who kept buckling and unbuckling her seatbelt. Such minor irritants could hardly stand in the way of true happiness!

By the time the refreshments trolley arrived, Jane's stomach was a mass of knots. She passed up the plastic cup of orange juice that would have tempted her twenty minutes earlier, and closed her eyes, inhaling and exhaling deeply and purposefully. Her nerves had clouded out all her earlier happiness. Her heart was pounding with such intensity that she felt it must be ready to burst through her chest.

The American woman had taken to repeatedly crinkling her plastic cup. Jane tutted loudly, despite herself. She was not one to cause a fuss. She considered herself the least non-confrontational of all her friends and family, but this woman had stretched her to the limit of her patience. She released all the oxygen from her lungs in one sharp, dramatic exhalation and stood up with such urgency that the women froze.

As Jane sashayed down the aisle to the toilets, a flight attendant smiled kindly at her. She had a pretty face under all the makeup she was contractually obliged to wear. Jane went into the restroom and closed the door with a little more force and volume than she had intended. She slid the door lock closed, and her eyes landed on her reflection in the small mirror. In the harsh overhead lighting, her skin appeared rough and mottled, the paper-thin skin under her eyes, more crepey than usual.

How would John react when greeted with this sorry sight? Why had she not made a hair appointment, instead of trusting Margaret's assurances that Jane's hair looked best when worn loose and slightly tousled? Margaret usually wore her long, mousy brown hair caught up in a bun, loosely braided, or tightly pulled back at the temples. She only ever wore it loose on special occasions, and it was long and flowing but without much volume at the crown. Jane would make a point of complimenting her on it.

When Jane arrived back at her seat, the American lady was fast asleep behind her oversized Gucci sunglasses with her head tipped back. Now that she was no longer obscuring her view, Jane saw that the man seated on the other side of her was William. He seemed to be engrossed by the in-flight magazine. She wondered if he had not seen her either, or whether he had seen her board and was snubbing her on purpose.

"William," she blurted as she took her seat.

He looked up. "Oh, hi!" The omission of her name and his neutral tone slightly wounded her pride. "Off to London? Well, of course you are!"

"Yes, yes," she muttered, trying to sound casual, feeling uncertain as to whether supplying more details would be oversharing. "You too? Ah, well, obviously." She slid back behind the human shield, who had woken up and was slipping a crystal into her bra.

"I'm going to visit my sister," William said.

As the American woman gripped the headrest of the seat in front and used it as leverage to push her bottom further back into her seat, Jane was met with the sight of a triangular patch of fresh sweat in the armpit of her green cardigan.

"I'd offer to swap seats with you so you can talk to your friend, but it takes me ever so long to get settled." The woman's voice was raspy.

"That's awfully kind. You're fine," Jane said, relieved. She could think of nothing more awkward. Whatever would they talk about?

"I'm Olivia," the woman announced, turning to William to proffer her hand.

Jane averted her gaze, pretending to search through her bag.

"How do you two know each other?" Olivia asked.

"Friends of friends," William clarified. "I'm William."

Jane felt relieved of the burden to converse with him. He had confirmed that they were, in fact, mere acquaintances. As William got acquainted with his new friend, Jane closed her eyes. Her stomach had settled. Would it be too late to ask the flight attendant for a glass of orange juice? She opened her eyes.

"Mint?" Olivia offered.

Jane quickly closed her eyes and pretended to sleep. She pictured herself walking in a park with John, and his daughter riding alongside on a tricycle. She couldn't believe she was flying to London to spend the night with someone she barely knew, who had predominated her romantic fantasies all her life.

She had heard of an Australian man whose relationship had sustained him throughout a ten-year prison sentence for armed robbery. When he was finally released, he couldn't bring himself to look at his girlfriend, so sickened was he by her face, once so beautiful to him. It had become wedded with the misery of obsession. Perhaps this would happen to her.

Eventually, she fell into a light sleep but was still aware of the movements of people around her. She could hear the flight attendant reassuring an elderly woman in front that there would be a wheelchair for her when they landed, and then, a few minutes later, that there would indeed be someone to push her. Olivia's breathing was becoming more laboured, the pitter-patter of conversation between her and William having died out.

Jane was jostled awake by the bumpy landing.

"My, oh my!" Olivia turned to look at William. "I was not expecting that!"

William chuckled. Jane felt strangely excluded. Why should she care?

"Would you mind, William?" Olivia said, gesturing at the overhead cabin.

"Oh, no problem at all. I can carry it for you."

Jane thought William's eagerness to please the older woman was endearing. Jane felt overlooked, but she couldn't allow herself the luxury of a negative thought. She had to emanate positivity and confidence when she walked into the Arrivals area, where John would be waiting with his hands in his pockets, looking devastatingly handsome, leaving William in the halfpenny place, as her mother would say.

Why were some women so good at getting men to do things for them? She wondered whether Olivia had been a beauty in her youth and still felt entitled to men's attention, and if William had picked up on this expectation on a subconscious level. Jane hoped that William would see John, so that he would know she could command a man's attention and that she was important and very much cared for by a really important man.

Jane and Olivia were two of the last passengers left standing at the baggage carousel. By the time Jane's suitcase appeared on the conveyor belt, William had long gone. She reached Arrivals on the heels of Olivia, who was immediately embraced by a tall, attractive man who kissed her deeply. John was nowhere to be seen. Jane walked casually through, as if she were expecting no one.

What the hell was she supposed to do? She searched in her carry-on bag for her phone. Had John brought her all the way to London just to stand her up? Had he cancelled via text message? Could he have forgotten she was coming or slept through his alarm? Had he even said he was picking her up? Her hands were shaking as she took her phone out of aeroplane mode.

"Jane!"

At the sound of his voice, she looked up. There he was, walking toward her with his hands in his pockets, smiling confidently.

Their time had finally arrived.

CHAPTER EIGHTEEN
Weekend in London

In the taxi to John's place in Islington, Jane was utterly charmed, though very little was said. They were each delighting in the other's presence and nothing more was needed. Jane, usually so self-conscious, felt her inhibitions drop. As she snuggled against the nape of his warm, muscular neck, she was a little surprised to catch a whiff of whiskey. He had probably been out for Christmas drinks the night before. When she reached for his hand, he grasped hers tightly.

When the taxi pulled up to the redbrick Victorian mid-terrace, Jane was pleasantly surprised. It was nothing as flashy as one might expect of a hotshot corporate lawyer turned stockbroker. This was the type of house in which she had always envisaged herself. She liked to be able to see right through a house and into its back garden. Just before Jane started secondary school, her parents had bought a large 1960s monstrosity, which they had extended sideways, backwards and upwards, as the pub became more commercially successful.

Upon entering the building, she walked headfirst into a stunningly beautiful woman who was effortlessly carrying a gravel bike down the stairs. She wore her shiny, waist-length hair in a low ponytail, and her tight grey leggings and dark blue sweatshirt with Japanese kanji emblazoned across the front made Jane feel ridiculously overdressed.

As the woman brushed past them on the stairs, she seemed to make a point of blanking John, and his overeager smile and the shrug of his shoulders made Jane wonder if there had once been something between the two. If she had a gorgeous, athletic neighbour of her own, wouldn't she have been the first to explore the possibility of romance?

Wasn't it better that he looked around and noted the full spectrum of beauty in his midst, and still chose Jane? She was someone's idea of exotic and mysterious, surely? The most handsome and sought-after men were often the most loyal; those with fewer opportunities were more likely to give in to temptation, should it come their way. Hadn't her mother always said that, and wasn't her mother wise in some matters?

The flat was sparsely decorated. The hall was dimly lit, and no photographs graced the walls. The sitting room furniture consisted of a rather uncomfortable-looking brown leather sofa, a large flatscreen TV, and an IKEA desk, piled high with paper files.

Jane perched on the arm of the sofa as he made his way to the fridge. She looked for evidence of his daughter – a trike, a few soft toys – but saw none. A whiskey bottle sat on the countertop, next to one half of a lemon and a sprinkling of cloves. It had the look of a medicinal preparation. Perhaps he had a cold coming on and had not been socialising after all. John produced a fresh bottle of prosecco from the fridge and closed the door. Fastened to the fridge door by a magnet was a photo of his daughter. She had piercing blue eyes, corkscrew curls, and a button nose.

He followed Jane's gaze. "That's Tilly! I showed you photos already, didn't I?" A look of pride suffused his features.

"Tell me about her!" Jane was genuinely interested, much to her own surprise.

"She's just turned three and three quarters, as she likes to tell everyone. And she's the funniest little thing, quite quirky. You'll meet her. Not this side of Christmas, though. She's with her mum."

"She sounds adorable." Jane had not expected to feel so overjoyed at the prospect of meeting her boyfriend's daughter. The fact that he foresaw a future with both her and Tilly in it delighted her. She brushed away any niggling concerns she'd had about his secretiveness. "Do you get to see her often?"

John rolled his eyes. "We're working all that out at the moment. Divorce – it's a messy business. Don't get married," he quipped.

"Don't worry, I won't!"

He poured two generous glasses of prosecco. She glanced at her watch. It was barely nine o'clock.

"What have you been up to since we last met?" he asked, leaning back against the counter and eyeing her up in a way that she would have found creepy, had he not been so handsome and successful.

"Oh, you know. Correcting. Slowly dying inside from the rubbish I have to read."

She squirmed, knowing that what she really had been doing was living in a sort of limbo as she awaited his invitation. She feared he'd given her very little thought. He hadn't bothered to ask her what subjects she taught but then again, maybe he presumed she would be teaching English. She felt as though she were a minor figure in his life, whereas he was front and centre in hers. Then again, he could equally be wondering why she hadn't enquired as to the type of investment banking he did.

He left the room and returned a minute later with a wine-coloured leatherbound photo album.

"Have a look," he said, handing her the bulging album.

It fell open to the centre page, which contained a photo of John and his ex-girlfriend, Dee. Surely, it was not his intention to remind her of all the women he had chosen over her. She feigned indifference as she leafed through the photographs. There he was, during his MBA year in Harvard, seated at a restaurant table alongside two impossibly good-looking women; hiking in the Alps, with a Swedish woman Jane could remember having seen about their hometown soon after graduation; and at Dee's wedding, with the pretty Asian woman who'd been his plus-one. How gracious of him to attend his ex-girlfriend's wedding. Why would he possibly want her to see this parade of the women in his life?

"Lovely captures," she said, her nonchalant tone belying the anger that coursed through her veins.

He smiled. When she arrived at the final page, she saw a barely recognisable image of herself standing between Sara and Dee, a head and shoulders above them. She looked statuesque, and her confident smile disguised how awkward she always felt in front of the camera. Had this photo prompted him to get back in touch? It was the only photograph that didn't feature John, and she realised he must have taken it himself.

She flashed back to the memory of him messing about with Dee's camera while they were all hanging out on the campus one afternoon.

Dee had brought along an engineering student called Eddie, who seemed to get on better with John than with Dee. As always, everyone except Jane hung on John's every word. She feigned her usual cool indifference. It had been the first time she caught John staring at her when she wasn't paying attention.

"A Titian beauty," he said wistfully and smiled, closing the album. "It seems quite fitting that you're on the last page."

Her cheeks flushed. Did John Davy really see her as being in the same league as all the conventional beauties that had graced the pages of his photo albums over the years? She gulped back the sparkling wine. Before she knew it, they were lying on the scratchy rug of his sitting room, her dress pushed up around her hips and her heart still pounding ecstatically in her chest.

She slept dreamlessly for a while and awoke to the sound of gentle knocking on the door of the apartment below. Infused with a sense of restful calm, she dared not move, in case she awakened John. Things, as they stood in that moment, were perfect. A change of any kind could jeopardise the radiant joy she now felt. If she could press the pause button at any moment in her life it would be now.

The future was full of potential pitfalls, revelations about John's past which would force her to relinquish the dream of a life with him. She would not tolerate a man who had cheated on his wife, whether casually or in the form of an intense long-term affair; she would forgive a myriad of other sins more easily than infidelity. Jane wasn't certain that he had cheated on his beautiful wife; she was merely fearful. But fear, in Jane's case, was all consuming.

Feeling a strong compulsion to ask him why his marriage had imploded, she placed her hand delicately on his upper arm and willed herself to shake him gently into wakefulness. She realised that in doing so, she would cast herself as being needy and overly invested in this relationship. She must continue to play the role of the insouciant lover.

Jane got up and changed out of her travel outfit. Taking style inspiration from John's understated neighbour, she pulled on a pink sleeveless blouse with ruffles at the shoulders and a pair of gunpowder-blue cord dungarees and tied her hair in a loose knot. The radio played classic hits from her teenage years as she tidied and scoured the kitchen counters. When John woke up, he rubbed his eyes in what she interpreted as disbelief. She caught a glimpse of her reflection in the microwave door. Her cheeks were rosy from the exertion of the housework.

"Dungarees! Now I remember what we used to call you," he said, pulling the plush grey blanket from the sofa and enfolding himself within it.

She bristled, and her cheeks flushed an even deeper shade of red. "What did you call me?"

He looked down. "It was stupid." There was something markedly pathetic about a balding, middle-aged man sitting naked on the floor. With the blanket draped loosely around his shoulders, he looked almost feminine.

She forced a teasing, jovial tone. "Now you have to say it!"

"Aw, come on," he said quietly.

"I'm sure it was all in fun," she said, somewhat unconvincingly.

"Crazy Jane. We had names for everyone! They meant nothing."

"I suppose you meant the weird, unhinged sort of crazy, as opposed to the fun and exciting sort."

"You were just different. Your clothes, your little ways."

She looked him directly in the eyes. "At least I was never boring, and predictably normal, like you." She turned up the volume on the radio. a song she was too young to remember.

"Different in a good way! You were creative and quirky."

She let the hot water run over her fingers before turning off the tap. "Let's go out. I'm starving," she barked.

"Does this mean I'm forgiven?" He began getting dressed. His plaintive expression melted any lingering frostiness on her part, and she filed away his comment for later analysis. "Do you like sushi?"

"I love it. I lived in Japan for a year, you know?"

"Did you?" He sounded genuinely surprised.

Had he never looked her up during the intervening years? The fact that she had been aware of his approximate geo-location at any given point over the preceding fifteen years made her feel stalkerish. It wasn't as if she'd been pining after him the entire time, but even when she and Daniel had been happily married (or so she had thought) she had still been curious about John's life. She felt that way about everyone, though.

When it came to men who had rejected her, she derived a certain satisfaction in seeing their relationships flounder. Every time John's status was changed to *single* on Facebook or she heard from a friend of a friend that his long-distance relationship hadn't stood the test of time or travel, she felt gratified.

"There's a great Japanese restaurant a few streets away," John said, buttoning his shirt. "Let's walk."

CHAPTER NINETEEN
At The Gate

Jane arrived at her boarding gate an hour early. John had put her in a taxi with so much time to spare that she had to wonder whether he was eager to be rid of her. She would have preferred that he accompany her to the airport and send her off properly, but at least he had prepaid the taxi fare using an app. He had kissed her somewhat distractedly on the cheek and made no mention of when they would next see each other, which sent her hurtling into the depths of despair. It was so close to Christmas, and they hadn't discussed their respective plans. Was it her turn to extend the invitation? She should have casually brought it up before she'd left, as texting him from the airport would reek of desperation.

Her thoughts turned to William, who would likely be on the same Sunday night flight back to Dublin. Jane scanned the lounge area. A woman with hollow cheeks bounced a toddler on her knee as her husband struggled to pry the lid off a Tupperware container. It came flying off, and yoghurt splattered everywhere, causing him to drop the spoon on the floor. She tutted, tossing him a packet of wet wipes. Jane turned to face the other way, aware that the man had no need for a second set of watchful eyes upon him. Had John and Liz been like this?

"Hello!" William had materialised before her.

As he rested his small sports bag on the ground and sat down, an elfin creature, with dark hair cut into a perfect bob, appeared and sat beside him. She studied Jane with a composed but accusatory stare.

"This is Natalie," William said, placing his arm around her shoulder. "Jane's a friend of a friend," he said to Natalie, giving her shoulder an affectionate squeeze before turning back to Jane. "How was your weekend?"

Natalie smiled meekly, edging closer to William. She had a petite and athletic build, well-defined bone structure, and large, grey eyes. Her plump, line-free skin could hardly be improved upon with makeup. Jane immediately considered the couple well-matched. It seemed ludicrous that she had expended so much energy on William, and his impressions of her, when he'd had a girlfriend all along.

"My weekend was just brilliant, thanks! We had the most fantastic sushi. And wasn't the weather amazing?" Jane babbled. Although she usually battled shyness when meeting people for the first time, she became almost ebullient in the company of someone far meeker than her. "How about yours? Did you get up to anything nice?"

"Yeah, I visited my sister, Annie. And I met Natalie's parents for the first time, which was lovely." He turned to Natalie, who looked sheepishly down at her feet.

"Will you spend Christmas in Ireland? Have you been before?" Jane directed these questions at Natalie, who she feared might not have any English.

"I'll be home with my parents in Birmingham for Christmas," Natalie said, but she had already returned her gaze to William.

"Yeah, it's just a flying visit," William added. "We only met in Dublin two weeks ago. Natalie has friends who recently moved to Notting Hill, so we decided to meet up while I was in London. It's been a bit of a whirlwind."

Jane felt a choking sensation at the base of her throat. Two weeks! William had really taken the initiative. It was truly impressive. If only John could take a leaf out of William's book. Since William had been single when Margaret introduced them, perhaps Jane hadn't misinterpreted his interest after all. She reminded herself that as he was now attached, and because she'd had no interest in him to begin with, his intentions or lack thereof, concerning her, were irrelevant.

"I came over to see my nephews before Christmas, and we babysat them while Annie went to her Christmas party. We didn't do a lot, but it was great to catch up," William said. "Whereabouts in London were you staying?"

"Islington." Jane willed him to ask with whom, but it seemed he was too courteous to pry. "Lovely neighbourhood, with sweet Victorian houses. I'd happily live there."

"I need a coffee," Natalie said dolefully, placing her hand territorially on William's forearm.

"Sorry, Natalie. I completely forgot." He turned to Jane. "Natalie's hurt her ankle, you see. I'm just going to run back to that coffee shop. Would you like a coffee?"

"A coffee would be lovely. Americano, please!" She had surprised herself with this request. She had no need for the effects of caffeine at this time of the afternoon.

Natalie took a book from her large handbag by a designer at the lower end of the scale, and began to read.

Determined to jumpstart the conversation before William returned, Jane asked her, "How is it?"

"Huh?" Natalie glanced up, frowning.

"I've heard good things about that book. Is it any good?"

"I don't know yet," Natalie muttered. By now, her features had set in a permanent scowl. "I've only just started it."

"Psychological thriller?" Jane enquired, nodding towards the telltale design on the cover.

Natalie affected to examine the image of the red Georgian door on the cover to avoid having to engage any further.

"*The Neighbour*," Jane sounded out the title. "They're so formulaic, aren't they?" She immediately regretted her remark, which had sounded condescending. "I mean, I love them. I just wish I could churn out a few myself."

She had irrevocably lost Natalie, who slid the book into her bag and folded her arms defiantly. Just then, William returned, and Jane gratefully received her coffee. As soon as he took his seat, Natalie turned away from Jane and engaged him in an intense and animated conversation that, as far as Jane could surmise, had no purpose except for monopolising his attention.

Jane pulled a paperback novel from her carry-on and read the same sentence fifteen times as her thoughts whirled a mile a minute. When she thought about her time with John, it was hard to say whether she had actually enjoyed herself. Boxes had been ticked. They had slept together. Rushed as it was, he seemed to have had a good time. They'd had two restaurant meals and watched a movie he'd streamed from an illegal website. He'd told her about his daughter, Tilly. Jane felt as though the relationship might finally be heading somewhere, now that they had started doing couply things. The visit had been a success in many respects, but she had been far too tense to fully enjoy it.

Margaret would ask her how the sex had been. She would give her friend an honest answer. It had been fun, and John had a very nice body, but she hadn't felt much. That was more about her. Jane had always had trouble reaching orgasm with a partner. Charlotte would want to know which restaurants they'd eaten at, if he'd paid for everything, and where his apartment was. Luckily, Jane had not revealed John's identity to her sister.

When they landed at Dublin Airport, William and Natalie promptly disembarked, leaving Jane stuck behind a woman with a difficult toddler, who refused to leave her seat. William and Natalie were going in the same general direction as she was. It seemed quite churlish of them not to have offered her a lift. She wanted more than anything to show William how fun and entertaining she was, compared with his insipid girlfriend. She recognised this urge as an attempt to distract herself from the grave misgivings she held about her own relationship.

CHAPTER TWENTY
Reflections

Christmas had come and gone. Jane had received a text from John on Christmas Day, late in the afternoon, promising that they would have their Christmas in January. Although he phoned every second day and spoke at length about Tilly, which was promising, Jane was consumed by the fear that he would soon tire of her.

While teaching had never been her calling, she had always enjoyed it, but ever since John had reappeared in her life last October, every last ounce of joy had been squeezed from her working day. If he didn't text to ask how her morning was going, she felt a sense of unbearable loss. As soon as their phone calls ended, she began to contemplate the loneliness she would feel if that were to be the last time they spoke.

Her evenings, which had previously been devoted to reading and writing, were now spent searching online for any trace of John's and Liz's happiness before their acrimonious divorce proceedings. She found a Wedding Bells announcement in the Times that Liz's parents had placed, and the one they'd placed themselves announcing Tilly's birth.

Jane revisited John's LinkedIn page, where he had a few thousand connections and a handful of recommendations. She had found a brief bio on the website of the legal firm where Liz worked. She was still using the surname Davy, which was likely a choice she had made to share a surname with her daughter. Her dark red lip, slicked back hair, and black suit were exactly what you'd expect from a successful corporate lawyer. She had a symmetrical face with bone structure as fine and delicate as that of a porcelain doll. Jane imagined she'd look a hundred times prettier if she tousled her hair and ditched the bold make-up and power suit. But who wants a corporate lawyer who's pretty, when you can have a cut-throat one? A group photo elsewhere on the website showed Liz standing next to three of her female colleagues, who all towered above her.

Jane had finished reading Olive Kitteridge just before her first date with John. She had picked up a few other books by the same author, including the sequel, but they held no appeal for her now. She promised herself that she would someday return to reading, and to aspiring to being a writer, but only after John had become a certainty in her life. She might even start to draw again.

Her moods were so up and down that there was very little pleasure to be found in what should have been the most exciting period of her life. She drank ginger tea to ease the nausea brought on by her anxiety. Charlotte joked that she was suffering from sympathetic morning sickness, but the truth was that Jane gave no thought to her sister or her sister's pregnancy. She had grown as self-absorbed as Charlotte, whose preoccupation with her own highs and lows Jane had always found despicable.

All her conversations with Margaret revolved around John.

"What you need is a distraction," Margaret observed, much to Jane's annoyance, as
she ladled two full teaspoons of artificial sugar into her milky tea.

Jane blushed. She had been dominating the conversation once again.

"I mean, you're not even happy, Jane. You've spent your whole life waiting for this man, or someone like him, and now you have him, and you spend your whole time worrying he'll lose interest and ghost you."

"I don't think he will, but my mind just goes into overdrive," Jane snapped defensively, embarrassed by her friend's painfully accurate portrayal of her situation.

She hated the idea that he'd gone out and lived his life in the intervening years, while she had been waiting for him, and dreaming of a chance encounter that would bring them together again. She had avoided men who reminded her of him.

Upon reflection, she could now see that Daniel had been the

opposite of John in every respect that mattered to her. It would have been too difficult to spend her life with a pale imitation of such an idealised figure. That was probably why things had worked with Daniel for so long. If she'd been emotionally invested in him or in the relationship, she might have seen the cracks sooner. She might have cared that his mind was elsewhere.

In retrospect, it was as if her heart had been asleep for that decade of her life. She had unconsciously chosen someone who would never fulfil her, because she didn't want to be fulfilled. Being fulfilled by another man would be a betrayal, not of John Davy but of herself and her adolescent notion of love.

"How are things with you and Frank going?" Jane almost immediately regretted her question.

Never, in all the time they had known each other, had Jane enquired as to the state of her friend's relationship. Margaret only ever revealed minor annoyances. She was the friend who listened but rarely shared. If there had been anything awry, she would most likely bottle it up. Jane fought to keep the corners of her mouth from turning up into a smile of nervous embarrassment. Her pettiness had overtaken her. To use her best friend's revelations about the reality of her own relationship against her, to drag up something shared in a moment of unprecedented openness and honesty was beneath Jane.

"Oh, Jane, that's a nasty question. You obviously have you your own thoughts on Frank and me."

Jane blushed a deep shade of red. Biting her lip, she burst into tears, releasing months of pent-up emotion and distress in one elongated sob. Margaret, never one to hold a grudge, put down her mug and wrapped her arms around her. Jane could not have expressed her regret more eloquently in words. Margaret squeezed her shoulder and pushed the plate of digestive biscuits in her direction. Jane knew she had been selfish and arrogant in thinking that her friend's relationship was somehow inferior to hers. Sure, there was nothing glamorous or exciting about Frank. He was distinctly average in every sense, and incredibly dull to Jane's mind, but he loved Margaret and made her happy.

"I'm sorry," Jane whispered, feeling quite exhausted. "I don't know why I said that."

"Oh, don't apologise. We have our little niggles, like all couples do. You'll see, when you and John move on to the next stage."

As usual, Margaret seamlessly bypassed any potential conflict.

Jane couldn't help but wonder if this was how she dealt with any of the so-called niggles in her relationship with Frank. It must be hard to fully clear the air if you're never prepared to show how you really feel. Cheered by her friend's optimism, Jane picked up a biscuit and bit into it. "Oh, that would be great."

Her mood decidedly more upbeat now, she drifted off into one of her delightful daydreams about her future life. She tried to imagine what that would look like. She pictured herself living with John in a beautifully appointed home. Tilly would visit at weekends. She painted the entire scene in her mind. John, watching as his beautiful new wife interacted effortlessly with his daughter, displaying a warmth and naturalness that he had never witnessed in his ex-wife. It would be wonderful if it actually materialised. But she couldn't summon any real excitement.

"We're having the housewarming next Saturday," Margaret said. "You should ask John along."

"Oh, I don't know if he'd come."

"I see!" Margaret's tone of mock offence irritated Jane.

"It's just that I don't feel as if we're at that stage yet, you know, where you introduce each other to your friends." Jane's mind immediately sprang to her airport encounter with William and Natalie. He had brought her home to introduce her to all and sundry after knowing her for all of two weeks.

"Who else is going?" Jane was suddenly eager to ascertain if William would be there.

"Frank's friends from college and work, and his sister. And some of the staff here."

Jane noted Margaret's reticence to refer to their colleagues as friends. The surprising thing about Margaret was that, despite her warmth and wit, she had very few friends. She had no trouble talking to people, including strangers. She was well-liked by all the teaching staff at St Mary's, but her acquaintanceships rarely developed into friendships. Jane was not exactly a friend magnet, either, but the people close to her fulfilled her in a way that twenty half-baked friends never would.

"Well, I might ask him if he rings tonight," Jane said. "Who knows?" She was already dreading the conversation, during which she would affect a breeziness that was not her own. If only she could borrow someone else's confidence for the duration of the call.

Just then, Michael McDonnell, a former science teacher, peeked around the staffroom door. He and Jane made fleeting eye contact, each afraid to acknowledge the other in case a hearty hug was required. Jane felt uncomfortable hugging most people, her family included. Michael and Jane had never gotten to know each other, and each found the other's icy demeanour unsettling. Jane hoped he'd slip away to the office downstairs, in search of a warmer welcome. Just as he was withdrawing his head from the gap in the door, Margaret turned her head and Michael's face lit up.

"Michael!" Margaret stood up and rushed toward the doorway with her arms outstretched.

"Mags, how are you?" Michael wrapped his arms around her with such enthusiasm that Jane felt compelled to avert her gaze.

When Margaret freed herself from the embrace, the two of them chatted for a while before he made his excuses. He had come to see his colleagues in the science department and went off to seek them out in the laboratories, which were all located in a modern block across the courtyard. Margaret turned to Jane with a look of curious mirth.

"And what was that all about, Mags?" Jane whispered upon hearing Michael take his first few heavy-footed steps down the ailing stairs.

Margaret smiled wryly. "I guess he missed me more than I knew."

"More than he knew!" Jane grinned. "I think he surprised himself."

Jane envied her friend's ability to put people at ease. Was it a skill one could learn? She felt uneasy and self-conscious whenever she tried to emulate the social grace that others so easily displayed.

"OK, I'm quite overcome now," Margaret said, pretending to fan her tears and smiling seraphically before gathering up a small number of history copies for a senior class.

Jane could imagine how much Margaret's small, senior year classes adored their teacher. She was punctilious and exacting with her junior classes, but by Fifth Year, she had weeded out the vapid types, who were devoid of opinion, and her classroom became a sanctum for the healthy exchange of views and informed debate.

On the other hand, Jane was a poor disciplinarian. She hated the whiny tone of her voice when she complained, and she feared that harping on about incomplete homework or forgotten books would turn her students off the subject. She tried to find something to praise in each one of them. Jane was not phoney; she was simply herself, the best version thereof, the one she wished she could present to everyone, especially to the men in her life.

The truth was that Jane was afraid of men – those who reminded her of her father, those who were his opposite, those she suspected might like her, those who held her in low regard. In essence, all of them. She felt distinctly uncomfortable around the opposite sex. She could think of no man with whom she'd happily chat. If there was one man who left her feeling fully at ease, might it be John? She nurtured the half-formed hope that if only she could let go of all her inhibitions and deep-seated insecurities, she and John could be wonderful together.

CHAPTER TWENTY-ONE
The Housewarming

The awful thing about make-up was that once you started applying it, there was always one more thing to add. Jane wasn't sure if she looked any better for it. Of course, she lacked experience and expertise in this area. She'd only ever been a mascara girl. For all she knew, her technique might be adding years and emphasising things that should be played down.

Margaret's housewarming had presented the perfect opportunity to invite John over to stay at hers. She had asked him somewhat tentatively, and he had immediately and enthusiastically taken her up on her offer.

She wondered whether there was enough time for her to re-wash her hair. The seventeen-year-old trainee stylist, who was the owner's niece, had looked blankly at her when she'd asked for a quite messy bun. Jane had once sat next to a sophisticated woman in a city centre salon who requested a hairstyle that looked as if she could have done it herself – a little undone, without being raggedy – and Jane had committed this description to memory.

The trainee stylist had nodded in agreement before consulting at length with her aunt in hushed tones in the far corner. Jane watched them closely in the mirror. The owner, a woman in her forties, wore an expression of utter confusion. Eventually, the trainee returned and proceeded to create the most perfectly boring French roll Jane could have ever imagined.

And here she was, four hours later, afraid to liberate her hair from its perfectly constructed roll, in case it ended up being demonstrably worse. The heavy-handed stylist had first smoothed out Jane's curls, leaving only the faintest kink at the end. Jane tended to look severe when her hair fell straight and flat around her face. It had long been her view that women with large crowns, such as herself, could not pull off poker-straight hair. Now that she examined her bone structure closely in the bathroom mirror, she wondered if it had more to do with the shape of her face, her prominent chin, and her jawline that was rather too delicate for her Roman nose and high cheekbones.

The doorbell trilled, jolting her from her reverie.

"Please don't be John," she muttered to herself.

But who else could it be? Number Four Mill Lane rarely attracted unannounced callers. Her neighbours were not the type to drop in to borrow a cup of sugar or an onion. She peered out through the bedroom window at the front of the house. A taxi was halfway through making a four-point turn on the narrow street outside. John Davy was walking up the path to her cottage, wearing the same type of blue gingham shirt and gunpowder-blue chinos he'd worn to the awards ceremony in college, when he'd come first in First Year Law and she'd taken the prize for Early Irish.

As she padded down the stairs, she recalled how he had leaned forward in his seat that day and nodded at her as she nervously sat five seats down from him. Jane had been overdressed in an ankle-length navy-blue tunic, which she'd bought with her mother in a shop on Grafton Street the Saturday before. The girl to her left, a natural blonde and delicate beauty who'd placed first in both History and English, had worn a jumper and jeans, having heard about the prize only that morning from her landlady. The invitation had been sent to her home address in Monaghan and her parents hadn't thought to open it.

Jane's parents had travelled up from Glin for the ceremony. Her mother, who was all done up like a wedding guest, was taking too many photos. Jane's father tugged awkwardly at the collar of his shirt. Jane had taken Early Irish along with a handful of Americans, most of whom were on exchange and not sitting exams. Her achievement was minor. She resented her mother for telling her she'd have to dress up. John had tied for first place with a girl who'd recently been in the running for the Attorney General's job.

Jane yanked open the stiff front door to a sight she thought she'd never be lucky enough to behold. John was standing in her doorway, beaming, oversized sports bag in hand.

"Hello, Jane. You OK? You look a bit distracted."

Jane smiled. "Of course!"

She was struck by the thought that if that beautiful blonde girl from the awards ceremony had opened the door to John, he'd have smiled as widely, if not more so. She thought of that sporty neighbour of his. Surely, he'd prefer to be seen with her on his arm. She was fully certain that most men would plump for either of those two classic beauties over pudgy old Jane, with her translucent skin and chubby thighs. She could feel her inner thighs rubbing against each other as she led John into her living room for the first time.

"This is where Jane Mythen lives!" He surveyed the living room approvingly. "Very nice!"

She went into the kitchen and had barely reached the fridge when she felt the weight of his arms around her waist. She turned and briefly embraced him before slipping from his grasp again.

"Happy Christmas, Jane," he murmured, nuzzling his head against her neck and pulling her back into his arms.

"Just let me pour us both a glass of wine," she said.

Why couldn't she imagine ever feeling fully at ease in this man's company without the aid of alcohol? She managed a few furtive sips before he took both glasses from her and set them down on the wooden coffee table. When he placed his hand firmly on her thigh, she feared this was leading somewhere she'd rather not go so early in the evening.

As disappointed as she'd been with her hair, she didn't want to arrive at Margaret's housewarming looking as if she'd been dragged through scrubland. She also had no desire for John, or for any man, when she was stone-cold sober. It was probably why she wasn't prone to the type of indiscretions other people were. She found it too easy to behave herself, never tempted to cheat or stray or wander off with some inappropriate stranger late at night.

She sat back in the sofa, taking another sip of her wine. He took the hint and reached for the TV remote control. The black and white image of a gaunt elderly man appeared on the screen.

"What's this?" John asked.

"Oh, now this will be right up your street. Bob Durst came from this incredibly wealthy real estate family from New York—"

He had flicked to the next channel before she'd even got to the interesting part, about the murdered friends and the months he had spent living as a mute nun in Texas. When John had perused the entire contents of her recordings library, he turned off the TV and carefully placed the remote control down between the wine glasses before lunging at her.

She pulled back. "What are you doing?" She was surprised by the assertiveness of her own voice. It was as if she was hearing someone else, someone stronger, speaking for the first time.

"What's wrong, Jane? Are you OK?" He leaned his head against her bosom, much in the way a child would against his mother's, which Jane found unusual but strangely endearing. "I'm sorry, Jane, did I offend you? I've just been dying to see you."

The concern in his voice made her feel she'd overreacted. Perhaps she had made far too big a deal of his poor conversational skills. Would she prefer that he pretended to listen intently, nodding in agreement while plotting how he could get her into bed at the earliest opportunity? At least he was open and honest. He could barely concentrate on what she was saying, such was the intensity of his desire for her. He was the type of man who loved to be in love. She wrapped her arms around him and squeezed him tightly, before suddenly jumping to her feet.

"I just need to touch up my makeup. I'll be two minutes."

In the bathroom, she looked at herself in the mirror. She had always thought that if she ever were to find a boyfriend again, he'd be interested in the same things as she was. He'd laugh at the same jokes and have a general appreciation for her humour. Not that she was hilarious, but she wasn't dull, either. She had plenty of opinions and ideas, but come to think of it, he had thus far shown very little interest in what she thought about things. Had he even asked her opinion on anything? He hadn't even thrown in a few closed questions. She ran the water for a few seconds and then went back into the sitting room. He had drained both glasses in the meantime.

By the time their taxi pulled up outside Margaret and Frank's newly renovated home on Seaview Close, John was slurring his words. He'd had only one glass of wine, admittedly a generous serving, before finishing off her glass. Was it possible he had been drunk on arrival but better able to disguise it than most? Had he had a few drinks on the plane or in the airport?

Margaret had spotted them through the bay window of the

sitting room and was there to greet them as they negotiated their way through the hallway, John noticeably unsteady on his feet. Jane hugged her friend tightly, squeezing her shoulder before drawing back to take in the loveliness of her appearance. Margaret's large hazel eyes were lined with purple kohl, and her cheekbones, lightly dusted with pink, had popped into sharp relief.

Jane suddenly remembered that, in her rush to get there, she'd forgotten to pick up a bottle of wine. For all his tipsiness, John managed to gush to the right extent and generally give the impression of being a successful and confident man. The small groups of men, deep in conversation about golf or politics, nodded to John as he trailed after Jane, who persisted in profusely apologising, despite Margaret insisting that there was no need for an apology or wine. No one seemed to notice that John was slightly slurring his words. Even Frank seemed taken in by his charm and good looks.

Before long, John had positioned himself at the centre of a large group of people, none of whom he'd met before, and was, without much apparent effort, leading the conversation, everyone hanging on his every word.

Margaret led Jane into the conservatory for a view of the back garden. They sat on a pair of wicker chairs.

"Will you keep this?" Jane gestured at the flimsy structure that encased them.

It was fine on dry days like this, but its single glazing could be no match for the spring rain that surely lay ahead.

"God, no. It'll be the first thing to go. His parents are going to sell the holiday home in Wexford."

Jane raised her eyebrows. Frank was the youngest son of a reasonably well-off Dublin family. She doubted they needed to sell off their little cottage to help him do up his first home. Margaret always felt the need to play down his family's wealth, as if Jane were some poor misfortunate who might be offended by the privilege of his upbringing. She felt like asking why they wouldn't get a loan. They had no mortgage. What couple in their thirties buys a large family home with their own money?

But it was Frank's house, she supposed. There was no immediate prospect of an engagement, no suggestion that either was interested in having children. Margaret studiously avoided any reference to whose house it was. She simply referred to it as The Rectory, which made the whole affair sound even more pretentious.

"It'd be nice in the summer to have somewhere to sit and read, if it's not warm enough to sit outside," Jane offered.

"I think we'll just extend the kitchen instead."

Jane stretched out her legs. "Well, I like it. I wish I had somewhere that got the sun like this. I'd be slow to get rid of it."

Margaret leaned back on her wicker chair and pushed the door closed. "He's lovely, Jane. He's very charming." Margaret nodded in the direction of John, whose back they could both see in the galley kitchen.

"Oh, I suppose he is. I really like him." This was something Jane knew to be true. She did really like him, she always had. He was handsome and smart, and he'd chosen her, over all the hundreds of women who'd happily take her place. And yet, she felt as if she were talking about a character in a TV series, someone she had once found attractive but had gone off. She looked over her shoulder to see John Davy talking to Margaret's most attractive friend, Corinne.

"Oh, God, what does Corinne want with him?" Jane caught sight of her furrowed brow in the window opposite. She consciously relaxed her forehead; aware she was likely to prematurely develop the deep frown lines that her mother had.

"Who knows? What does Corinne want with any man? Attention," Margaret wryly observed.

"I don't know how you put up with her. She just adores herself. It's sickening."

Margaret shrugged. "Men like her. I don't know why, either. She's not even that pretty!"

They both laughed. Corinne was too good-looking, her features so perfectly formed, her bone structure delicate, her teeth impossibly white and straight, and her legs long and lithe. They couldn't take her seriously. She had no substance. She was always a whole chapter behind the conversation, and she would laugh at her own, infuriatingly silly jokes. It was a great way to filter out the undiscerning men. Any man worth his salt would extricate himself from her grips within ten minutes, anyone who willingly stayed didn't deserve to be rescued.

Jane finished off her glass of wine, hopeful that when she strained her neck a little to the left, she'd see John chatting happily to anyone other than Corinne.

"What's wrong?" Margaret turned to see the source of Jane's discontent. "Oh, don't mind her, she's just like a child in a sweet shop."

Corinne stared up at the strapping young man, as her boyfriend draped his arm protectively over her shoulder. Jane considered Corinne's boyfriend a simpleton. Any man who could enjoy spending time with someone that vacuous had to have some glaring want in his character.

Miriam came in and joined them, pulling up a wicker chair to sit between the two friends. She was tall and slim, with a build that Jane would enviously describe as willowy. She was married to a friend of Frank's. How peculiar, Jane thought, that Frank was the one with all the friends, and Margaret, with her warmth and humour, was almost entirely dependent on him for social interaction. He was, for some baffling reason, good at making and keeping friends. It didn't make sense.

"Do you mind if I smoke, girls?" Miriam was already rustling through her oversized handbag for a lighter.

"Of course not. I've given up, though," Margaret added.

Jane wasn't sure she liked being addressed as a *girl*. Having spent too long in Japan, Miriam had taken on the mannerisms of her American colleagues at the University of Tokyo, where she had taught an extramural English class. She was rumoured to have had her own show on a local TV station, where she chatted with other expats about their experience of Japanese culture. She would naturally have enjoyed celebrity status.

Jane had lived in a small industrial city further north. Despite her height and flaming locks, she had passed unnoticed through the city's streets. Working as an English language tutor in a busy city centre school in Koriyama had been the refuge she sought in the aftermath of her separation from Daniel. Carmel, the previous principal of St Mary's, had kindly granted her a one-year sabbatical in consideration of her circumstances. Her mother had fielded frequent calls from Daniel, who demanded that she put the apartment on the market or renegotiate the rental arrangement she'd agreed with Charlotte, who had moved in with Neil. Jane resented hearing of Miriam's popularity when she had floated invisibly through that period of her life.

Margaret reached for the wine bottle that sat on the glass-topped table before them and refilled Miriam's glass.

"Margaret, I love this place. The location, it's to die for."

Miriam's husband appeared and touched her gently on the shoulder. Bryan was greying around the temples and was better-looking than Miriam but had considerably less charm. She seemed to understand the reason for this delicate interruption. Without uttering a word, she fished in her bag. Margaret intuited that Miriam was looking for the lighter, which lay on the table. She handed it directly to him. He mouthed *thank you* before disappearing as seamlessly as he'd arrived.

"So, what do we think of Pat's new girl?" Miriam was never afraid of a dramatic U-turn.

Jane's interest was piqued. "Who's Pat, again?"

Miriam gulped back her wine, belching with such a lack of inhibition that Jane wondered if she'd imagined it. Miriam showed her gums when she smiled, and the way she crinkled her nose when listening intensely made her look like a ferret. Jane glanced over at Bryan, who certainly was far more conventionally attractive.

Jane remembered seeing their wedding photos on Margaret's phone. Miriam had worn a strong red lipstick, which she had carried off very well. Jane had almost seen why Bryan considered himself so lucky and to be *punching*, as Miriam liked to remind him and everyone around them after a few drinks. At first, Jane had thought she was aiming for sarcasm, a brutally honest acknowledgement of the disparity in their looks, but from the way that she spoke about herself and the male attention she had received in Japan, it became apparent that she truly regarded herself as a raving beauty. Despite this conceitedness, Jane liked her.

"Oh, look who it is!" Margaret stood up, flinging her arms wide, her eyes narrowed, her stomach thrown forward in an unflattering stance.

To Jane's surprise, Miriam jumped to her feet as well. Jane turned to see William smiling profusely. He was accompanied by Natalie, who looked self-assured and quietly confident. Smug, even. Jane now recalled Margaret having mentioned that William, Bryan and Frank had shared a flat or a house in college. They were an unlikely trio: William, affable; Frank, harsh and critical; and Bryan, vanilla. Next to William, Bryan seemed grey and lifeless.

Margaret and Miriam both hugged William, then Natalie, who accepted their embrace less enthusiastically. Jane remained awkwardly rooted to her seat, waiting for the greetings to end. Miriam pushed her seat back and motioned for them to join the circle. Jane was waiting for William to acknowledge her. Natalie studiously avoided her gaze.

Margaret and William dragged two more wicker chairs over from the far side of the conservatory. Natalie smiled meekly, and William laid his hand gently on her shoulder as he enquired as to her choice of drink.

"A beer, please."

Miriam lit a fresh cigarette before shaking the box at Natalie, who shook her head.

"So, Natalie, you've been over a few times to Dublin now?"

Natalie looked stoically ahead, nodding but continuing to move items around in her loose canvas bag, giving the impression she was only there on sufferance.

"Where did you two meet?" Miriam's eyes widened in anticipation of a long and interesting story.

"Oh, you know, out. I was in a pub with friends. I was visiting." She seemed to have found what she was looking for, a scrap of tissue which she used to gently blow her nose.

William returned with two opened bottles of beer and handed one to Natalie. She turned her chair to face his, leaving Jane awkwardly cut off from the circle.

"Hi, Jane!" William moved his chair back so that he could talk to her.

Natalie's back stiffened. Margaret seemed to sense Natalie's unease and tried to draw her into the conversation they had been having about Pat's new girlfriend.

"Oh, I don't know Pat," she snapped, bringing the conversation to an abrupt end, without feeling any compunction to redirect it or reintroduce a new topic.

Jane noticed a momentary flash of annoyance cross Margaret's usually composed features. Natalie had shut down what would have been an intriguing story, and Jane loved a good story, especially one told by Margaret, even if she didn't know the protagonists personally.

"Well, Natalie, remind me to introduce you two later," Margaret declared in a retaliatory tone.

Jane liked it when her friends, especially her very good ones, disliked the same people she did.

"Are you still going back and forth to London?" William was saying. "I haven't seen you on any recent flights."

Jane hoped that John would eventually remember that he had come to the party with her. She could spy Corinne's fiancé standing in the kitchen and chatting to Frank, apparently unconcerned by his fiancé's overt fascination with another man.

Margaret suddenly asked, "Where's John?"

Jane would have preferred John appear naturally by her side. Telling people your good news never felt as satisfying as their witnessing it for themselves. But John was apparently too engrossed in conversation with Corinne to bother with his girlfriend. She felt strange even thinking that word: *girlfriend*. She certainly would never refer to herself this way in John's presence.

She scanned William's face for a micro-expression that might convey his regret at not having seized his opportunity when she was available. But he displayed no emotion, instead following Natalie with his gaze as she politely excused herself to use the bathroom. His attentiveness to his girlfriend irritated her, but only because the man who was supposed to pay her attention was too busy making new friends to bother with his old one. He had always been that way, as far back as she could remember. Nothing pleased him more than to meet someone new and to work his charms on them. She craned her neck to drain the last of the wine from the glass in what she knew could not be a flattering pose. What did she care? William only had eyes for Natalie.

As if reading her mind, Margaret stood abruptly. "Jane, would you like to see the curtains?"

Jane jumped to her feet too eagerly, feeling suddenly lightheaded. She steadied herself on the glass table before stepping over numerous oversized handbags to follow her friend inside, through the kitchen. To her surprise, Corinne had moved on to Frank's handsome older brother, who appeared distinctly uncomfortable with the attention.

He was newly separated from his wife. Jane knew this because Margaret had offered to fix Jane up with him. Jane had shuddered at the thought. He was awkwardly shy, with an irritating habit of talking out of the left side of his mouth. He wore short-sleeved shirts, like a supermarket manager, and buckled shoes. She cast her eyes quickly in the direction of the floor. Yes, there they were, the same old battered, buckled shoes.

Making her way through the kitchen and out into the hall, she cast her eyes about for John. Her greatest fear was that she'd find him collapsed on the sofa in a drunken stupor. They walked through the sitting room into the dining room, then out onto the porch, where a man stood with his back to them, smoking.

"Sorry, Pat." Margaret stepped around him gingerly, as if she were encroaching on his space.

He nodded, apparently too taken with a frumpy woman in a sleeveless dress and stepped haircut to acknowledge them.

"Who's she?" Jane hissed, when they were out of earshot.

"Let's just walk out to the gate. I'll show you this cute little post box that the previous owners erected."

Margaret and Jane exchanged a knowing look.

"She's a fucking ignorant groupie who has bewitched Pat Daly, mind, body and soul."

"He seems a ponce, Margaret. Were they talking to you earlier? They acted like there was no need to say hello," Jane said.

"No, not at all. That's the way they always are. He could be at my wedding, and he'd barely give me the time of day. She's been hanging on the outskirts of that group for years. Her sister was in their class in college for a while and she's been waiting for her chance with Pat for years."

"What does he see in her? I mean, that hair!"

Margaret accepted the cigarette that Jane proffered. She was grateful that Jane knew better than to bring up her earlier avowal regarding cigarettes. She knew well how alcohol could loosen one's resolve.

"Oh, they're a pair of pretentious bolloxes," Margaret's language became markedly less gracious when she drank.

She seemed, to Jane's trained eye, to be on about her fifth glass of wine. It was the drunkest she'd seen Margaret in a long time. Her left eye was flickering slightly, and her speech was hesitant and more drawn out. She pretended to walk down an imaginary staircase while muttering the words *one step, two step,* which was all the funnier because she was normally not one to express her humour through gesture or slapstick.

"Get up, Margaret!" As she tried to hoist her friend back up by the elbow, a large splash of white wine escaped the glass and landed on the shirred bodice of Jane's beautiful green dress.

"I was just giving a nod to her hairstyle," Margaret whispered conspiratorially.

"Oh stop, she'll know. It's so obvious you're mocking her hair." Jane peered over Margaret's shoulder to find Pat and his lady friend standing with their backs to them now. He was pointing at something, and her face was turned adoringly towards him, marvelling at something Jane couldn't quite get.

Pat was handsome in a goofy, long-faced way. His hair was balding on the crown and receding at the temples. He was tall, but his limbs were short and stubby relative to his elongated trunk. Worst of all, his hands were delicate and small.

"What are they looking at?"

Margaret spun around, "God knows. She seems to think he has a beautiful mind. He's probably pointing out some common-or-garden wren, and she's lapping it up."

Jane snickered. "Does he?"

"Does he what?" Margaret tipped back her head to get the last drop of the wine.

"Is he smart?" Jane loved to guess at people's motivations for acting the way they did. In Pat's case, pretentious and annoying.

"No! God, no!" Margaret practically spat out her wine. "He's a roadie. He travels around moving furniture on film sets and describes himself as a set designer on LinkedIn."

"No, really? Why would he do that when you all know he's a roadie?"

"Oh, Jane, you have no idea. He has, in my opinion, a personality disorder."

"Really? How does that manifest?"

"Well, he actually broke into our friends' house and stole their TV. They're his friends, too."

"What? Who are they?"

"Dearbhail and Charles. They're here tonight!"

Jane felt a strong desire to rejoin the main party and meet the full cast of characters currently taking form in her imagination.

"The redhead in the kitchen, and the guy she's here with," Margaret whispered conspiratorially, despite there being no one within earshot.

Jane had indeed seen them on her way in. As one of the only two redhaired women at the party, she had immediately sized herself up against Dearbhail. Her Titian-like hair, magnificently piled upon her head, was a more striking shade of red, and her complexion milkier. Although her features were not as handsome or as regular as Jane's, she had the feline quality, slightly upturned nose, and winsome grin adored by men.

"He tried to be a concert promoter or something like that. He knew Christy Dignam, and in fairness to him, got him to perform in a little festival in his hometown. But that says more about Christy than him."

Aslan had always been a favourite band of both Jane's and Margaret's.

"I've always loved Christy. But I met Billy once, and he was lovely," Jane said, referring to the band's guitarist, whom a college friend had dragged down from the stage at a concert in the Red Cow Inn a good ten years prior to this.

"You met Billy? He's so cool." Margaret was in danger of veering off topic.

"Yeah, so, Pat – why did he want a TV so badly?"

"I dunno. Maybe he really wanted to watch the omnibus of Eastenders." Margaret tittered at her own joke.

It struck Jane herself as odd that her boundless curiosity about strangers, such as Pat, did not extend to the people in her life who really mattered. She was aware of an unwillingness on her part to scratch the surface of John's character. It was an act of self-preservation. She had a sense that something dark lurked not far beneath the surface. She resisted Margaret's attempts to help her untangle the weeds, preferring instead to keep her focus on the pretty flowers.

"So, how are things going with John? Is he enjoying the party?"

"I don't know where the bloody hell he is! He's moved on from Corinne, though."

"Jane." Margaret's tone seemed condescending. "He came with you."

"Oh! And I'm supposed to be grateful that he's coming home with me, too, even though he'd rather talk to any other woman at the party except for me."

"Don't be a twit! How much have you had to drink?"

"Me?" The sharp edge to Jane's voice took both her and Margaret by surprise.

"C'mon, c'mon. Let's see where this handsome devil is!" Margaret dragged Jane by the elbow, in through the porch and down the long narrow hall. "Hmm, he's not in the kitchen!"

In any other situation, Jane would have found her friend's running commentary hilarious, but the combination of wine consumed too quickly, and weeks of repressed emotions had roused a beast that rarely showed its face. Although she knew better, Jane began to feel as if her best friend in the world were mocking her, as she danced about the kitchen, pulling open drawers, looking behind curtains, and asking party guests if they'd seen a tall financial analyst.

Only when Dearbhail whispered, "Stop it," casting her eyes in Jane's direction and then back at Margaret, did Margaret realise that her attempts to assuage her friend's anxiety had fallen flat.

By now, the tears were streaming freely down Jane's cheeks. It was ridiculous. She wasn't even that upset about John. Things were going better than she'd anticipated. He was here, visiting her for the entire weekend, out with her friends. Why was she crying in public? In front of strangers and near-strangers, who probably knew snatches of her back story: single, a bit dotty, stuck up, divorced, delusional.

This was awful. Everyone staring at her, Frank's friends looking on in abject horror, frozen with embarrassment but grateful not to be expected to react, happy to leave it to someone else's emotionally intelligent other half; and Dearbhail, the better-looking redhead – the type whose complexion stayed milky, and whose eyes didn't redden when she cried – rubbing Jane's arm.

"Jane!" John swooped in and caught her by the elbow. "Where have you been all my life?"

It was the kind of thing only John could say and get away with. It was cheesy, he was cheesy, and not as funny as he thought, but it somehow shifted the attention from her to him. He stood between her and the rest of the occupants of the kitchen, eclipsing her, as if holding a towel around her as she changed into bathing clothes on a beach. As he embraced her, she felt the tension leave her body. Here he was, supporting her in public. She had achieved what she feared she might not. They were a couple.

Margaret fussed about, refilling Jane's glass and making sure she had a seat at the table. She asked William to move back to widen the circle and make room for another wicker chair, which she dragged from a corner. John was too drunk by then to be of much help. William extended his hand to introduce himself and Natalie. John muttered something unintelligible.

Jane noticed how lovely William looked in his crisply ironed sky-blue shirt. His face was boyish and soft, but his regal nose lent it an air of masculinity. When William complimented her dress, John placed a proprietary hand on her shoulder, agreeing that it was indeed a very pretty item of clothing. She knew John hadn't even noticed her dress, but she was reassured by his need to stake his claim.

"Did Corinne get her claws into you?" Miriam teased. She spoke to John as if she knew him intimately, and yet, as far as Jane was aware, they had never been introduced.

John had that effect on people. They would always take the mickey, knowing that attractive people are used to being paid a lot of attention, and will respond favourably. He chuckled, and Miriam smiled widely, revealing for the first time her new dental veneers. Jane sensed that John was more taken with her than he had been with Corinne. Perhaps Miriam had not overstated the extent of male attention she received.

John removed his arm from Jane's shoulder. William was happily relaying what must have been a mildly entertaining story about traversing through Customs with an uncle with a metal hip replacement. Natalie looked on stony-faced, but Miriam chuckled, dividing her eye contact equally between the two men. She drew strength from male attention. Next to her, Jane felt listless and opaque. She was envious of Miriam's confidence.

John tilted his head towards hers. "Another drink?"

Jane noticed that his hand had been resting on the small of her back all this time. He was so gracious and considerate. In that moment, she wouldn't have cared if Miriam had done tumbles and cartwheels for his attention. She sat, unfazed, completely secure in his affections. "Maybe a Coke, please. We'll probably go after this."

Miriam craned her neck to see where he had disappeared to, chagrined that their conversation had been cut short. William became the sole focus of her attention. She laughed loudly and licked her lips like some predatory insect, waiting for her moment to pounce.

"So, Natalie, how did you two meet, again?" Jane asked. "Was William hanging out at the bar alone?"

Natalie cast a sidelong glance at William, who noticed her discomfort and answered the question for her. "I was there alone, waiting for a friend, and Natalie took pity on me."

She smiled weakly, clearly grateful to be rescued. He leaned in and kissed her on the cheek before turning back to Jane. "So, John's a really nice guy."

"Thanks." Jane was strangely disappointed.

She was happy to hear that John was liked, but she had wanted William not to like him too much. His lack of jealousy seemed to indicate that he hadn't had romantic feelings for her. Or, perhaps he was pragmatic, and moved on quickly.

From the corner of her eye, she saw John emerging from the kitchen. Margaret had slipped away and was now standing on the outskirts of a small group in the garden, hovering nervously with a platter, completely unconfident in her culinary efforts, insisting she would take no offence if they didn't like her vol-au-vents.

"How are things at St Mary's? Do you have exam classes?" William asked with his eyes fixed firmly on Jane.

She registered a fleeting look of annoyance cross Natalie's face, and the almost imperceptible tug that she gave his shirt sleeve. It was the gesture of an insecure schoolgirl and made Jane even more determined to give his question her full attention, not so much to rouse John's jealousy as Natalie's.

"Oh, yes. Every year." Jane was reminded of the fact that John had not asked her a single question about her work.

"I hear you're very good," William said, nodding in Margaret's direction.

"She says that about everyone! It's what all the really gifted people say, don't you find?"

He paused, considering her words carefully. "You mean, really gifted people praise people who aren't so great?"

The awkwardness of his words made her smile. "Gee, thanks, William. Say what you really feel."

"I said I'd heard you were good. Very good, in fact." His shoulders shook gently as he laughed.

Feeling tickled that John would overhear her being described as a talented teacher, she hoped it would rouse his interest in her career. She was eager for William to elaborate. John was perched upon the arm of her chair, having offered up his seat to Margaret, who happily slid in beside Jane. He showed no interest in the conversation at hand. He must not have heard the compliment.

"I was useless at writing essays," William said modestly. "I don't think I handed one in for the whole of Sixth Year."

"Didn't the teacher mind?" Jane was suddenly distracted by how handsome William was, noting again his strong nose, almond-shaped eyes, and reassuringly natural smile.

John had had substantial work done on his teeth. They were all capped, as far as she could tell. He had lost the sharp jaw of his youth, and a roll of fat had settled comfortably around his stomach. His shiny watch, undoubtedly incredibly expensive, seemed a little tight on his wrist, a bulge of fat between its strap and the cuff of his crisp shirt evidence of the luxurious business lunches he was expected to indulge in. His father, too, had developed a large paunch in midlife.

"I was the bane of his life. He ended up giving me an essay to learn off before the exams, and I just wrote it down verbatim."

"Was it on topic?"

"I didn't care, Jane. It was the essay they were getting, regardless of the title, and I passed."

"What was it about?" Jane's curiosity surprised her. There

was something engaging and funny about this man that she hadn't noticed before.

He rolled his eyes dramatically, which caused her to laugh. "Oh, God knows. Something about Pythagoras."

"What? The maths guy? You wove him into an English essay?"

"I wish I had it now. I'd love to see what you'd make of it."

Jane was flattered by his interest in her opinion, but she noticed that John had started to chat with Natalie. She had worked hard for John Davy, she wasn't going to let William's limpet of a girlfriend enjoy one minute of his company. She tuned out William's voice, intent on catching the thread of conversation between their respective partners. As usual, Natalie was giving very little, just smiling, which was progress for her. Not even Natalie was immune to John's charms. He mentioned something about Leicester.

"Did you go to college there, Natalie?" Jane had no interest whatsoever in the answer to this question, but she was determined to insert herself into their conversation.

"No, I went to UCL."

As nothing about her response invited further discussion, Jane decided that she had better try another tack. "Oh, well, John lives in London," she offered, knowing full well that he would have already shared this most basic of facts.

John was making no effort to bring her into their tête-à-tête. Feeling a mixture of humiliation and annoyance, she turned to William, whose eyes were still fixed firmly on her. He was not a jealous man. He acknowledged that John was the superior male, and no doubt anticipated Natalie's obvious attraction to him, but he was secure in himself and trusted his girlfriend, feeling no need to monitor her every move. Jane wished she were similarly secure.

"What are you drinking, Will? I mean – William." She giggled.

"You can call me Will."

She decided to redouble her efforts at rousing John's jealousy, seeing as he was so engrossed in his conversation with Natalie.

"Heineken." He stood. "Would you like one?"

"No thanks, you're good. We're going soon!" She raised her voice, in hopes that John would hear.

"Let me fill you up. Is that your wine glass?" Margaret leaned over Jane's shoulder and proceeded to fill the empty glass that sat next to her glass of Coke.

As discreetly as she could, Jane glanced back and forth from

William to John. If she were meeting them both for the first time, long, lithe William with his blue peplum shirt and slightly sallow skin, would have been more to her liking. But wasn't this proof of how first impressions can be so misleading?

William was fine, courteous and amiable, but he was not at all intriguing. They had no connection, no shared past. She would never have noticed him if Margaret had not tried to shoehorn him into her life. How had her discerning and sensitive friend judged him a suitable match for her? Now that she thought about it, Natalie was a perfect fit for him. They both were conventionally good-looking, and dull as ditchwater.

When Margaret offered to refill John's glass, he winked at Jane, and whispered, "One for the road!"

The prospect of having him to herself again buoyed her spirits. It was still early and bright enough for them to sit out in her small back garden and chat. She was too tired to drink any more. She returned to the kitchen to make herself a double espresso with Frank's fancy coffee machine. Nabbing the last remaining vol-au-vent from a plate on the sideboard, she carefully made her way back to John's side.

He turned to acknowledge her, as if not expecting such an imminent return. Shaking his head slowly from side to side in mock disbelief, he said, "She just can't get enough of the stuff."

"I thought you hated coffee, Jane." William had turned to face her.

She smiled, the bitter aftertaste of her least favourite beverage lingering longer than she'd hoped.

"You're right. I bloody hate the stuff."

"It does the trick, though, doesn't it?"

There was something in the way he smiled at her that made her feel just as she had the first time they'd met at the coffee machine in the staffroom in St Mary's. It was as if he was taking her all in, not in a lascivious way, but rather in an innocent, open-hearted one, a boy looking at her in wonder, with a mixture of admiration and awe.

And there it was again, that same micro-gesture from earlier, Natalie tugging sharply at the arm of his shirt to signal her disapproval. But this time, he didn't step to attention. He pulled free instead, his eyes still firmly fixed on the soft contours of Jane's mouth as she suppressed a smile. She could feel her cheeks flush.

John drained the last drop of wine from his glass. Unaware of what stirred within him, he knew that his position was somehow precarious. William was no longer safe, at least in his eyes. He stood abruptly to leave, smiling graciously at the others seated around the table. Jane fumbled with her bag, excusing herself, thanking Margaret, trying to make fleeting eye contact with everyone at the table, not wanting to offend anyone. Margaret fussed over them, offering to book a taxi, wondering if they wanted a coffee.

Miriam, as if on cue, glided across the patio and into the sunroom. She had been monitoring them closely from afar. With outstretched arms, a smile already fully formed, she gave the impression she and John were lifelong friends. He kissed her cheek, and she laughed in acknowledgement of his attraction to her, as if to say, *I know you find me desirable but we're both taken*. Jane could imagine Miriam, at some not-too-distant point in the future, telling a group of women she barely knew how there had been an instant attraction between the pair but that neither of them would act upon it. Her joy at having inadvertently stirred John's jealousy was immediately dampened by this exchange.

"I must give you a few business tips next time we meet." This was a nod to their earlier conversation about his having attended Harvard Business School. "Sign you up to our MBA."

John guffawed loudly. "I could probably learn a lot from you, Miriam."

She turned to Jane, crinkling her nose. "We're launching a whole suite of master's degrees next year. I mean, insurance, phone plans, you name it. Tesco is taking over!"

Jane suddenly remembered that Miriam had a senior role in the marketing department of the major retailer. She presumed this joke to be an attempt to flatter John, being the bigwig that he was. It could have been funny, Tesco sidestepping into Masters' programmes, cornering the market in education. The notion of John, who held postgraduate degrees from Cambridge and Harvard, signing up to study with a supermarket chain was funny. The inference that he might learn more from them than he had in all the other hallowed halls of educational institutions would, under other circumstances, have tickled her. She would probably have joined in on the joke, asked if he could use Clubcard points against his college fees, if she hadn't been quite so furious at Miriam.

"We'd knock the rough edges off you, John."

"You are just as charming as you are insulting." His smooth delivery of what sounded to Jane like a rip-off of a Woody Allen quotation made her feel certain this was not the first time he'd used the line.

"How very Oscar Wilde of you, John!" Miriam grabbed Jane's forearm and whispered in her ear, her breath a mixture of nicotine and wine, "Hold on to him!"

Jane wriggled free from Miriam's grip and directed her attention towards Margaret, who informed her that the taxi had arrived. Frank was now standing at his girlfriend's side.

"Thanks so much for coming." Frank proffered his hand to John, who shook it vigorously, patting him firmly on the shoulder.

He kissed Jane awkwardly on the cheek before Margaret walked them both to the door.

"We love the place!" Jane called over her shoulder as she ran to the waiting taxi.

They sat in silence on the journey home. The words had just slipped out. The *we* felt forced. Had Margaret winced at the use of the plural pronoun? Jane looked out of her window, furious that John would allow Miriam to think he was enthralled by her. Her feelings on the status of their relationship changed from one moment to the next. In one moment, she sensed that they were on the path to marriage, and in the next, she felt like his mistress.

"Where in France is Corinne from?" John mused aloud.

Jane rolled her eyes dramatically, sighing so emphatically that the taxi driver glanced over his shoulder. "Corinne is not from bloody France. She's Irish, but she's just really thick and she went to boarding school in Dublin with a load of international students, so she has this weird hybrid accent."

John laughed. "Why was she talking so much about the place then? Nice this, Bordeaux that."

"Her name's not even Corinne! It's Karen."

He laughed again.

"I made that up, but it wouldn't surprise me if it was true."

"So, she's not at all French?"

"Nope! No French grandmother lurking in the attic. She just likes to give the impression that she's French. She won't correct you if you wrongly presume."

"What a looper! When I asked her if she missed the French weather, she said no, she didn't."

"That's Corinne for you, John. She wasn't going to put you right. She's the most annoying of Margaret's friends. I don't even think she considers her a friend."

"Hmm." He peered out the window. "Too funny!"

Jane feared that she'd gone too far, perhaps he considered her last comment catty and unnecessary. Wasn't a woman's bitchiness about other women perceived as jealousy or insecurity? Margaret was so much more tolerant than her. She vowed to find something positive to say about another woman there. "Miriam is great fun, isn't she? I wish I got to see more of her."

"Yes, she certainly is. She's a very impressive woman."

Jane winced at his word choice. Miriam had no qualms about letting you know she had been promoted over her husband, despite only being in the company a wet week. Marketing was not Jane's area, so she had no way of telling if Miriam really was as superb as she made out. The way she licked her lips, God, it was disgusting. Jane didn't care what her work rate or output was, or how she outpaced her more senior male colleagues. Truly brilliant people did not need to advertise their success or worth. Bragging was never impressive. She was bursting to share her latest insight, but she bit her lip. She had said enough for one taxi journey.

"Home at last!" John kicked off his shoes and stretched back on the sofa.

The same John Davy who had placed first in his graduating class of Law in UCD and attended Oxford on a Rhodes scholarship, viewed as home her tumbledown labourer's cottage in poor man's Greystones.

"Come here, sit down next to me, Jane." He opened his arms.

Melting at the mention of her name, she fell effortlessly into his embrace.

"You are," – he held her back so he could appraise her beauty more fully – "divine."

Although she winced at his word choice, wondering if this was a compliment he paid all women, the word sparked the tiniest flame of optimism in her heart once more. It was as if her actual feelings toward him were muted. She had no way of telling if she was about to topple head over heels or if she was already firmly in love with this man. She was certain this was a result of self-preservation rather than apathy. Who wants to stoke a hope that will probably be dashed, anyway?

She got up and went to the kitchen to fetch some wine. Back in late August, she had stood in assembly on the first day of yet another school year, after a summer of unsuccessful first dates, and felt that she would be single forever. Never would she have contemplated being here in her little cottage with John Davy all to herself. It seemed incomprehensible that her luck could change so dramatically within the space of a few months. It was so difficult to live in the moment and enjoy whatever this was, when she had a non-stop commentary running in the background.

By the time she returned to place two newly filled glasses of white wine on the oak coffee table, she could hear the peaceful rise and fall of his breath. She examined him in repose. His features were not as defined as she'd remembered, the sides of his mouth slightly downturned, his hair thinning on top. But none of these things mattered a damn if you had known someone in their youth, when their chiselled looks and natural charisma had marked them out for great things. A little hair loss, and a soft paunch where once there had been a washboard stomach, had not deterred Corinne or Miriam in their efforts to charm him. She wrapped her arm around his middle and laid her head upon his chest, and the beating of his heart lulled her into a deep and restful sleep of her own.

CHAPTER TWENTY-TWO
A Cosy Sunday

Jane awoke, alone in her bed, to the sun streaming through the window and the sound of the cheap coffee machine chugging furiously below. She wondered whether John was preparing breakfast or just having a quick coffee before rushing off to the airport. Hadn't he mentioned that his flight was later tonight? Perhaps he planned to visit Clodagh and her kids before returning to London. More than anything, she wanted to have him to herself for the entire day.

She donned her Japanese dressing gown and an air of nonchalance that she hoped would suit her just as well and breezed into the kitchenette.

He looked up from his phone, smiling broadly. "Good morning!"

She forced a yawn, stretching her arms overhead, feeling unsure as to how to respond to his hearty greeting. She longed to wrap her arms around his neck, but she couldn't risk appearing needy. Everything was going so well. Would she have felt this way with any other man? She wondered whether she ever would feel fully at ease in his company. Surely, with time, she'd shed her self-consciousness.

She could imagine how his ex-wife, Liz, might have draped herself around him. With her perfect bob and tiny waist, she was not the type of woman to second-guess a man's interest. This self-assurance was probably what made her irresistible to men. And then, John was behind her, wrapping his arms around her not-so-fragile waist and pulling her towards him, which chased off any insecurities that were rattling around in her head.

"Fancy some breakfast? Perhaps some eggs?" She disliked having any cooked food before noon, but she relished the opportunity to spend more time in John's company.

"Yes, please. Should we go out? I saw a nice café—"

"No need. I'll whip us up some scrambled eggs. We have all the ingredients."

They seemed to have drawn a little closer together the previous evening. Today would be the day they got to know one another properly. She was eager to get a window into his past, and she wouldn't mind having some idea of his intentions. This afternoon, she would ask all the questions she had been dying to ask him for quite some time now. Were the two of them exclusive at this point? What had happened between John and his ex-wife? Was marriage now completely off the table? As much as she dreaded learning the answers to all these questions, she was equally unwilling to wait until her next visit to London. It would undoubtedly take some Dutch courage, but she was not averse to having a glass or two of wine over lunch.

She wanted to feel like they were a couple, and part of this was having other people see them as such. She envied couples who appeared in each other's social media avatars. John's Facebook profile picture had remained unchanged since his MBA graduation from Harvard. It wasn't even all that flattering. If he hadn't updated it when he got married or when his daughter was born, he was hardly going to put up a photo of himself with Jane.

The taste and smell of butter in the eggs was overpowering. It was why she never ate the cooked breakfast in hotels. The cup of tea he had made her was weak and milky. When he mentioned offhand that he would be visiting his parents in Glin, her heart sank.

"You're going to Limerick today?" Jane asked him, trying to hide her disappointment that her plans to ply him with alcohol and get him talking were scuppered. "I thought you were flying out of Dublin late tonight."

"I am! I was talking about going up to visit my parents sometime before Easter, in case you'd like to join me."

"Oh! Sure. If you'd like me to."

She had her answer right there. He was as serious as could be.

They had been dating for only a few months, and he was bringing her home to meet the parents. Had he already told them about her? She had no need for any promises or commitments when she had received the royal invitation to the Davy household.

The rest of the day passed in a blissful haze. They spent the afternoon watching TV in companionable silence. Jane loved nothing more than to sit inside on a sunny day. She was strange like that, she knew it. They took a short nap in each other's arms. There was something delightful about snoozing on a sofa bathed in golden sunlight, the warm glow from the mid-afternoon sun lulling them into a meditative state. They returned briefly to the bedroom, before ordering in some Indian takeaway. He was in a taxi headed to the airport by 6 p.m.

CHAPTER TWENTY-THREE
A Visit from Charlotte

Charlotte had come to visit, but only because Neil was away in Liverpool, where he was considering opening a costume outlet. Charlotte was listing out all the reasons why Liverpool was the perfect fit when Jane's phone beeped. It was Sara.

Call me! Lots to tell! Hope all's well. S.

Jane usually was not one to avoid uncomfortable truths. She preferred to be fully apprised of all the facts before jumping into anything. And yet, she couldn't bring herself to answer Sara's text message about their long overdue lunch date. Even the most amicable of splits have grisly tales. Although John and Liz probably hadn't completely gone to war over the custody of Tilly or the division of assets, Sara was sure to have found out something that would paint John in an unfavourable light. Jane knew that she would have to deal with whatever dark tales her friend had uncovered. Sara had a dramatic streak and loved more than anything to be the one to impart news, good and bad.

The information recently acquired by Sara had to be something bad. Who has something positive to say about the breakup of a marriage? Perhaps it was simply news of their impending divorce, or a disagreement about where Tilly would spend her next school holidays.

Jane concluded that the tone of Sara's message was far too light and breezy to be anything too negative.

Could Liz and John possibly be amongst the very few couples in the world who had managed to disentangle from each other's lives amicably, without the attendant acrimony and in-fighting that are part and parcel of the divorce process? What was it people said about divorce lawyers? They see good people at their worst. Anything was possible, Jane supposed, especially when it came to John Davy.

"What's up, Jane?" Charlotte queried. "You're in a world of your own." She continuously rubbed her hand back and forth over her bump, much to Jane's annoyance.

Jane decided to play it down. "It's nothing. Just that I'm well overdue to have lunch with Sara, and I can't think how I'll fit it in before Friday."

"Why? What's on Friday?"

Jane balked. She had no intention of telling her sister how she planned to spend the following weekend.

"How's Sara doing, anyway?" Charlotte didn't seem to notice that her question had been left unanswered.

"She has two boys and is working her way through her parental leave. Her husband's a consultant in Beaumont now."

"Oh, that Marcus! He's such a bore!" Charlotte rested both hands on her stomach and inhaled deeply. "He always gave me the creeps."

"It's Gordon. Where'd you get Marcus from?"

"God, but he looks like a Marcus! Didn't you tell me he looks like he's been left too long in the bath?"

"What?" Jane had, in fact, said that, but she feigned ignorance. "As a child?"

"You know what I mean! You used those very words to describe Ronan Keating. It's like, squeaky clean, rosy cheeks, translucent skin."

"Did I? You're right, though. He does look a little like Ronan, but better looking, obviously." She didn't really think so, but her loyalty to Sara compelled her to defend him somewhat from Charlotte's excoriating appraisal.

"Can I come and see Sara with you?" Charlotte asked sweetly.

Jane was taken aback. Charlotte had never shown any interest in any of Jane's friends before. "Why?" she blurted.

Charlotte abruptly stopped rubbing her bump. "Oh, that's nice." She pursed her lips like a scolded child.

"I didn't mean anything by it. Just – is there any special reason you want to see her all of a sudden?"

Charlotte widened her eyes in annoyance. "No, Jane. No reason. Just that it might be nice to see Sara again, but if you don't want me there—"

"Don't be silly. I'm sure Sara would love it."

"Great! Well, I'm free on Tuesday and Thursday nights," Charlotte chirped, scrolling through her phone.

Jane nodded. "I'll send you some possible dates tomorrow. I'm so busy with mock exams and corrections over the next few weeks, but we'll figure something out."

She had no intention of having Charlotte anywhere near that conversation. Charlotte was dying for everyone to know her pregnancy news. Jane doubted that her sister had any interest in seeing someone she'd always looked down on. Scruffy, she'd called her. If only Charlotte could see Sara now.

CHAPTER TWENTY-FOUR
Friday Night

That Friday evening upon landing, Jane had taken her phone out of aeroplane mode to see a text from John telling her to hop in a taxi and come straight to his flat. She presumed he was working late and that she would walk into his apartment to find him in the midst of a phone call with a client in Tokyo. Instead, she found the front door slightly ajar. She set down her luggage in the hallway and tentatively entered the sitting room to find him sitting barefoot on the sofa with an almost empty glass of whiskey.

"Sorry!" He rattled some remnants of ice in the bottom of a glass at her. "I started earlier than usual."

As unimpressed as she might have been, she was nevertheless reluctant to start the weekend on a sour note. She went into the bathroom, which was barely larger than the one you'd find on most domestic flights. Once inside, she inhaled deeply several times, not taking as much care with her exhalations. She hadn't eaten since lunch, and she could feel her hands shake, a sign that her blood sugar was low. Catching her reflection in the mirror, she was surprised to note her clear complexion, and two perfectly rounded circles of pink sitting high on her cheekbones. Had she slept particularly soundly the night before or was her radiance a trick of the artificial light?

"Red or white?" John called from the kitchenette.

"Surprise me!" she snapped back.

She re-applied the chalky roll-on deodorant she'd bought in the airport and dabbed several dots of concealer in her nostril creases before emerging from the bathroom. John seemed to have sensed her dismay at the lacklustre welcome and was fussing in the kitchen in a desperate attempt to rustle something up. He emerged two minutes later, holding a plate on which he'd scattered four animal crackers, two Hobnobs, and a handful of raisins.

"Sorry, Jane, I'm shockingly unprepared for adult visitors," he said, smiling apologetically.

She reminded herself that many men would be the same. It was simply not in their nature to plan ahead or to buy in fancy nibbles for their visiting girlfriends. Was it wrong that Jane longed to be the person whose preferences he considered when selecting biscuits or breakfast cereal? Was it selfish of her to wish that he would plan their weekends together as meticulously as he did his days out with Tilly? Perhaps it wasn't so much that he was treating her as an afterthought, but rather, he saw her as being a low-maintenance girlfriend and he liked that about her. While all his energy was being consumed by co-parenting, divorce negotiations, and work, Jane was the one part of his life that was easy, that he didn't need to think about.

She knew John had a lot on his mind these days. He'd been leaning heavily on his business partner for months now. One night over the phone, he had confessed to Jane that James O'Halloran had been carrying him since his life imploded eighteen months ago. She imagined his drinking didn't help. Suddenly, her hurt gave way to pity. He became once more a poor and wounded boy in her eyes, desperately missing his daughter, a devoted father cut loose by a fickle and cold wife.

As Jane ate her kindergarten snacks, John informed her of what he had planned for the weekend. The following afternoon, they would be going to Cheeky Monkeys Hoddesdon. When Jane enquired as to whether this was a trendy bar, John informed her that it was the soft play centre where Tilly's fourth birthday party would be taking place. John went on to reassure Jane that Liz would not be in the least bit put out by Jane's presence at this event, from which Jane grasped that her attendance was required. Jane looked at her watch. It was half past eight. All the shops were closed.

"Oh God, why didn't you tell me sooner? I would have gotten her a present."

What was she saying? The man who wouldn't even think to buy a supermarket baguette and some pre-sliced Emmenthal cheese in advance of her arrival from another country would not understand that children's birthday gifts did not simply materialise out of thin air. Was this the kind of husband John had been? She entertained a brief fantasy about getting trashed on a girls' night out with Liz and getting to the heart of it.

"What does she like? Maybe I can pick up something tomorrow." As the words came out of her mouth, it dawned on her that she had shown no interest in Tilly until now. She had not asked or even wondered about the child's personality or interests.

"Oh, don't worry, Jane! She won't be expecting you to bring her anything."

"Maybe we can share the gift you got her," Jane suggested meekly.

John's less-than-enthusiastic grunt caused her to wonder whether she had overstepped the mark. He went on to say that having Jane there would make it feel less awkward for Liz, who would be bringing her new boyfriend, Desmond. John made a point of raising his eyebrows and smiling goofily each time he mentioned Desmond's name, perhaps to indicate that he harboured no jealousy towards him.

Jane was daunted by the prospect of meeting Tilly for the first time in front of a watchful, nosy crowd of her fellow preschoolers' parents, who were au fait with the backstory and might be curious to see the next chapter of the drama play out in real time. But who was she to think she would even figure in the proceedings? How natural it was for Jane to don the cape of invisibility! If anyone could show up at their boyfriend's child's party and fail to ruffle any feathers, it would be Jane.

Feeling herself start to spiral, she lifted her wine glass and gulped down her first taste of freedom. Within seconds, she could feel the alcohol kick in. Her body began to feel gloriously lighter, and the sharp edge of her insecurity softened. It was as if she were looking down at herself, perched on the precipice of a new life with the wonderfully handsome John Davy. What on earth was she so worried about? Things were looking better than ever. Life held so much promise.

CHAPTER TWENTY-FIVE
Cheeky Monkeys

The mothers at the party all huddled around Liz in an arc formation, a fortress protecting her against John. Jane had correctly divined their frostiness. Why had John brought her along? Nobody had wanted her there, least of all his four-year-old daughter. One woman tutted in disapproval as John tried to break through the barricade to reach his daughter, who had her arms wrapped tightly around her mother's legs.

Liz was even more beautiful in real life. *Just a little overwhelmed!* Liz mouthed these words to the woman standing to her left, who was clearly her sister. They both had whittled waists, impossibly thin arms, and similar features set within the same face shape, only arranged slightly differently. Both made an equally pleasing impression. Jane felt humongous in proximity to them.

Seeming entirely indifferent to her unease, John left her standing on the outskirts of the group of approximately fifteen adults. Liz took Jane's carefully wrapped gift and placed it on the table along with all the other gifts. Upon realizing that her father had arrived, Tilly took him by the hand to give him a tour of the various slides and trampolines.

Jane looked around for a coffee stand, so she would be able to busy herself with queueing, rooting in her bag for change, and sipping.

The café was upstairs. She could see the assorted mothers with their unflattering Wigwam pants and unbrushed hair, sauntering with Styrofoam cups in hand to the play area where the children ran wild. Jane was a duck out of water. She took off in the direction of the stairs, hoping the queue would keep her long enough for John to miss her.

The English were an unfriendly lot, she thought. From her new vantage point at the top of the stairs, she could make out John in the distance. The children had gathered around him and were showering him with attention, exactly as adults tended to do. She felt a twinge of jealousy. He was unconcerned by the awkwardness of her situation as the new girlfriend, alone at a family party, greatly outnumbered by his ex's friends and general allies.

She should have stayed at home. It seemed as though John had brought her along only to prove to Liz that he, too, had moved on. Where was Desmond? Of course he wouldn't be there. Liz was far too mature to parade her new boyfriend around in front of her ex. Unlike John, she had nothing to prove to anyone.

Jane delayed her return to the group for as long as possible, pretending to marvel at the sight of little children chasing each other wildly in and out of soft tunnels. The humiliation of attending a party where she was unwanted and unwelcome transported her to the disco in the local tennis club twenty years earlier, when she had stood on the outskirts of a group of fashion-conscious teenagers while her own sister pretended not to see her.

She had known Charlotte wouldn't want to have her there, since they weren't really friends. Their father's encouragement had been well-intentioned, but Jane regretted having listened to him. She tried to bring the memory into sharper focus. Had she left early? If so, how had she gotten home? She was certain that the episode hadn't ended well. It was around this time that she realised that life was not fair and just, and that the events of her life would not mirror those of the romantic heroines she so loved to read about.

A middle-aged woman in a blue gingham sundress touched her lightly on the elbow. "Tea, dear? Or coffee?"

"I'm sorted," Jane replied, raising her plastic cup for the woman to see. "But thank you so much for asking."

"Not at all!" The woman smiled, and her sparkling blue eyes crinkled at the corners. She seemed to be wearing very little makeup, if any at all. She had fair, Gallic features and faintly lined, glowing skin. Her strawberry-blonde hair was silvering around the temples.

John eventually rejoined Jane, locking eyes with her so intensely that she felt it was part of a performance for someone else's benefit. He leaned in close, almost whispering in her ear, his hand hovering at the small of her back, as he complimented Jane on her dress.

Every so often, John would move into Liz's orbit in response to a subtle nod of her head or a glance in his direction. When the woman with the strawberry-blonde hair appeared with a large, iced cake topped with a unicorn and four candles, John stepped forward. Liz squeezed Tilly's shoulder, and the little girl beamed up at her mother before returning her gaze to the cake. John patted the strawberry-blonde woman on the upper back, and she turned to acknowledge him with a warm smile. The ease of their interaction gave Jane the impression that this woman must be Liz's mother.

There seemed to be no obvious animosity between John and Liz. Why couldn't more couples bring their married life to a close in such an amicable manner? John hovered behind the inner circle, who sang cheerily to Tilly. After Tilly blew out the candles in four swift breaths, John affectionately ruffled her hair before extending his hand to Jane, who reluctantly took it.

As the final ten minutes of soft play was announced over the loudspeaker, general pandemonium ensued. Later, as the parents queued up to collect their children's shoes from reception, and the other parents, who hadn't stayed to help with supervision, arrived to pick up their children, John graciously greeted them and engaged them in small talk, seeming eager to correct any negative impressions of him that they might have formed.

The women were totally charmed by John. She knew he had no romantic interest in any of these women, and this made his need for validation seem even more pathetic. In the midst of this awkward co-parenting situation, his priority was ensuring that everyone knew he was a nice guy. What did it matter what the other parents, whom he'd see only once or twice a year at similar events, thought? He was preoccupied with curating his perfect image, rather than making Jane feel at ease in this deeply uncomfortable situation.

As they pulled out from the industrial park that was home to Cheeky Monkeys, the woman who might be Liz's mother waved enthusiastically at them.

"She's friendly," Jane prompted.

"Yes, she is. She's a lovely woman."

Jane was becoming increasingly frustrated with his unwillingness to share information. "Well, are you going to tell me who she is?" she snapped.

"Oh, I beg your pardon, Jane. I thought I saw you two chatting." His smooth delivery and calm tone made her aware she was overreacting.

"Barely anyone spoke to me, John. Not even you." She was unable to recover her equanimity quite as easily as she'd have liked. "I mean, who was going to want to be seen showing interest in me, with Liz there? What could I have done to fit in with them? What was the point of me even being there?"

He placed his hand on her thigh. It was warm and suffused her with a sense of calm.

"I don't know anything about your situation," Jane continued. "Didn't you think it was odd that I was there at your daughter's birthday party, and I never spoke to her?"

"I wasn't thinking about you, I'm sorry. I was quite concerned about Tilly, to be honest. She's become very different from how she was before Liz and I split up. She's a lot shyer."

Jane bit her lip, feeling ashamed. She was making it all about her, when John had every right to prioritise Tilly. The fact he had communicated this in such a gracious and gentle way made her feel all the worse. "I'm sorry. That was really gross of me."

"Oh, Jane, you could never be gross. You're just sensitive. Tilly's a lot like you, in that sense."

Jane's heart was ablaze with love. She usually detested it when others described her as sensitive. It usually meant you were shy, inhibited, and not much fun. To be called sensitive by John Davy, who saw it as an admirable trait, and to be compared with his daughter, whom he dearly cherished, brought Jane immeasurable satisfaction. She could envisage a future with all three of them in it.

John would be driving, Jane in the passenger seat, occasionally glancing over her shoulder at the little girl lost in a book – *Mallory Towers*, or *The Worst Witch*, her own childhood favourites. Fresh from the ferry at Cherbourg, they would make the three-hour journey to the little gîte she'd found online the previous year. Tilly would have a special connection to Jane that was different from the bond she shared with her parents. As she grew up, Tilly would come to Jane when she was exasperated with her parents or afraid to share something with them for fear of their reaction. Jane would be the cool stepmother, who felt no need to control Tilly's life in any way. Even Liz would quietly respect her from afar and value her judgement.

"Any idea of how you'd like to spend the afternoon, Jane?" John asked, drumming his fingers on the steering wheel and shooting her a sidelong glance.

She tried to suppress a smirk.

"Oh, I just read your mind," he said, placing one hand firmly on her thigh and squeezing it. "I like the way you think."

She smiled and looked out of the window. She had a very clear idea, and it involved chilled wine, slow and generous lovemaking, and falling asleep in each other's arms.

CHAPTER TWENTY-SIX
Revelations

When Margaret suggested catching up over one of their leisurely weekend lunches at the little Italian restaurant in Greystones, Jane had assumed it would be just the two of them. As the black Volkswagen Golf pulled up outside her cottage, Jane was surprised to discern someone riding in the passenger seat. The sheen upon the window's surface obscured the person's features, and Jane thought for a moment it was a woman before realising that it was Frank.

She climbed into the backseat, and he acknowledged her with his usual measured greeting. Frank kept his gaze planted firmly on the road ahead as they sped away. While the two women chatted rather less easily than usual, due, in no small part, to his presence, Jane waited patiently for mention of his plans for the afternoon. Surely, they were dropping him off somewhere along the way and he would not be accompanying them to the restaurant.

Alas, he was still sitting in the passenger seat when Margaret wildly reversed the car into what was not, technically speaking, a parking space outside Rosetti's.

"Are you sure we're allowed to park here? It's a parking bay, no?" Jane enquired innocently.

As a rule, she did not reverse or parallel park on busy streets or when anyone else was around. Margaret was perfectly happy to let a queue of irritated drivers build in her wake as she manoeuvred her way into a too-small space. She did not hear Jane's enquiry; such was the level of concentration required for the task.

The three of them entered the restaurant in silence. The waitress offered them a table by the window. Margaret took a seat, Jane sat opposite her, and Frank made the somewhat awkward choice of sitting next to Jane. A gentle piano version of an old Frank Sinatra tune tinkled on a sound system from behind the reception desk, where a pleasant-looking, middle-aged Italian woman tapped out a text message on her phone with the tips of her long, red nails. Frank gave the menu his undivided attention as Jane and Margaret reminisced about having eaten lunch here the previous August, just before the dreaded school return.

When the waitress arrived, Frank barked out his order, then glared pointedly at Jane with a look that closely resembled contempt.

"Oh God, my turn!" Jane yelped. She had been far too busy chatting and soaking up the atmosphere to peruse the options.

Margaret could be relied upon to make her choice spontaneously and without much forethought. Unlike Jane, who was still haunted to some degree by the disordered eating of her teens and twenties, Margaret had a delightfully carefree relationship with food. Nothing was ever off limits for her. She pitied those whose fitness goals and fear of weight gain restricted their choices and curtailed their pleasure. She was enviably comfortable in her skin and proud of her undulating curves. Absently running her hand along her soft belly, she requested the carbonara.

"I'll just have a pizza. The smallest size, please." Jane had a faraway look in her eyes, as she struggled to decide between pepperoni and ham.

The waitress pursed her lips and narrowed her eyes impatiently. "So, ham?"

"Pepperoni! No, on second thoughts, make that ham!"

Margaret broke into that easy laugh of hers as Frank furrowed his brow, examining the drinks menu as if his life depended on it.

"And to drink?" the waitress enquired.

"That I do know. One of your passionfruit martinis, please." Jane looked across the table at Margaret.

"Ah, I'm driving, but maybe Frank will join you."

"I'll have a glass of Sauvignon Blanc. New Zealand."

He cleared his throat and Jane noted something awry in his

demeanour. He was acting more dour than usual, if that was even possible. Jane was so distracted by his pained expression that she missed Margaret's drink order. When she returned her gaze to her friend, she found her grinning broadly in an artificial way. Frank's knotted brow and Margaret's foolish grin made Jane certain that they were about to announce their engagement. The thought of her best friend being tethered to this misfortunate for the rest of her life filled her with undiluted dread.

"Jane—" Margaret began. She cleared her throat. "I have lung cancer. We've caught it early, so Frank and I have decided to get married."

"What?" Jane spluttered in disbelief. Words eluded her.

"Yes!" Margaret smiled sympathetically, as if Jane were the one with the diagnosis hanging over her head. "It's stage two, and we're not without hope, but we'd like to do it while I'm relatively healthy." She composed her features into calm alignment, but her eyes watered nonetheless, betraying her terror. A steady stream of tears, so perfect they looked artificial, meandered down her cheeks. One of them sploshed on the laminated drinks menu the waitress had forgotten to collect.

Jane placed her hand on Margaret's surprisingly sinewy hand, noticing for the first time how thin her friend's wrists had become.

"We've come to terms with it," Margaret said gently.

Frank tensed his shoulders, in defiance of this statement. There was nothing about Frank's manner that spoke to peace or acceptance.

"So, what's the course of treatment? You're so young—"

"I'll be starting chemo in the next few weeks."

Frank looked Jane squarely in the eye. "There are treatments abroad we are looking at—"

"No!" Margaret protested. "My mind is made up. My consultant has said that I have a decent chance of remission—"

Frank cut her off. "We have the money to go outside of this health system."

His family had the type of money at their disposal that would give Margaret access to cutting-edge treatments and top-notch medical professionals. The faraway look in Margaret's eyes told Jane that despite her protestations to the contrary, she had not fully made peace with her situation.

The waitress appeared, holding a martini glass and a wine glass by their delicate stems. She placed them carefully on the table. Jane nodded her thanks. Frank's mouth twitched rapidly from side to side.

"So, you'll start chemotherapy soon?"

"Yes, yes." Margaret nodded enthusiastically, looking to Frank for his approval. "In the next couple of weeks."

Frank was not buoyed by her attempts at reassurance. He looked off into the distance, his features deflated. Jane raised the cocktail glass to her lips and with her first sip, a tiny rose petal caught in her throat, before eventually sliding down to her already sickening stomach.

CHAPTER TWENTY-SEVEN
Plus One

If this were a balanced and normal relationship between two emotionally secure people, she would have phoned John by now, Jane thought. They had been dating for nearly four months, and she was forever waiting for him to make the first move. But this was different. The circumstances required her to call him. Her very best friend in the world – perhaps her only true friend – was getting married in June. If Jane couldn't even ask John to accompany her to the wedding, then what did that mean about their relationship?

The phone rang for an interminably long time before going to voicemail. Jane tossed her phone onto the pink chair that was positioned by the window and climbed under the covers. Her first thought ran to his gorgeous downstairs neighbour. Why would John stoop to Jane's level when he had a far more classically beautiful woman right there, literally, on his doorstep? The story she'd been feeding herself for the last few months about the strength of their connection and the intertwining of their fates had been flimsy, at best. If he cheated on her, things would at least make sense. Sure, she would be heartbroken, but there was something comforting in having your worst fears confirmed. You couldn't be tripped up if the most dreadful outcome had already happened and you had correctly divined it.

The shrill ringing of her phone summoned her from the comfort of her warm duvet. Her heart blossomed like a flower receiving water and sunlight after a cold, dark spell. Seeing his name on the screen obliterated her anxieties in an instant. Within the space of seconds, she found herself transported from the depths of despair to the heady embrace of euphoria. He was not in the arms of his beautiful neighbour. He had simply missed her call and was now returning it. She was his priority. She rejoiced; her thoughts were the only enemy here.

"John, it's about Margaret—" She caught herself. She realised she couldn't bring herself to share the news about Margaret's diagnosis in that moment. "Yeah, she and Frank are getting married on June ninth! Can you make it?"

"This June?"

"Yes. I guess you're probably busy?" She was grateful he could not see her now, with her flushed cheeks.

"It's awfully short notice. Let me have a think about it and come back to you. Liz and I haven't nailed down our custody arrangement. When the divorce comes through, everything will be clearer."

Once again, she had completely forgotten about Tilly. "I'm so sorry. I'm so stupid, I never even considered—"

"Come off it," he snapped. "No one's calling you stupid."

But she felt that she was. Not for forgetting about the very existence of Tilly, but for presuming that John would put her first. Yes, it was selfish, but surely, in the early flushes of a relationship, even the most devoted of parents had to make time for themselves. Shouldn't her best friend's wedding be significant enough for him to rejig his schedule for once? "Don't worry! You can think about it and get back to me." She injected every ounce of nonchalance she could muster into her delivery of that sentence.

"I'll be back the first weekend in April, a little ahead of schedule. Book me into Number Four Mill Lane! You still on for coming home to meet the folks? I'm home for five days, so we could make the trip down to Glin. If you can get a bit of time off work, that is."

"I'll figure it out," she said breezily. "We can do the weekend, at least. I can always come back early on the bus."

"Yeah, yeah. Sounds good. And I'll let you know about June," he added, without double-checking the date.

The conversation proceeded in the usual way, with John listing all the kinds of busy he was going to be over the coming week and neglecting to ask her anything about what was new in her world. She longed to share the news about Margaret's diagnosis and to hear some comforting words, but she feared that mentioning it now would seem like emotional blackmail.

As they said their goodbyes, John promised, as he always did, that they'd talk soon. Jane knew better than to expect a call in the coming days. After hanging up, she felt a lump form at the base of her throat. It was a feeling she knew well.

CHAPTER TWENTY-EIGHT
Exposure

The restaurant was busy for a Wednesday afternoon. Jane was debating whether to go for the Dublin Bay prawns when Sara appeared in the doorway of the large, carpeted upstairs dining room. She carried her younger son awkwardly on her hip while steering the older one towards Jane's table. The waitress carried Sara's large blue canvas bag, smiling meekly by way of apology for dragging her to the least accessible corner of the restaurant.

When Sara's irritation manifested as a slight twitching of her eyes, Jane noted her mistake and jumped promptly to her feet, taking Sara's weighty carry-all from the waitress. She tried to take the older child by the hand, but he recoiled in horror, burying his head deep in his mother's skirt. Were all children as deeply unpleasant as Sara's? She hoped that John's daughter was less prickly, she couldn't imagine him having an unfriendly child, though. And Tilly had seemed perfectly pleasant at her party.

Jane was apprehensive about this lunch date. Things had gone so unbelievably well the last time she visited John. She feared that Sara might unintentionally say something that would dampen Jane's hopes for her fledgling romance. John had been making it a habit to call her every few days and had even started to ask questions about the staff members whose names came up often in her gripes about life at St Mary's.

"How's Gordon? Is he working today?"

It was a ridiculous question. Of course he was working. It was a weekday. Jane hated the insincerity that rang in her voice. Surely, Sara would detect that Jane had no interest in Sara's family. Did that make Jane a bad person? She reckoned it made her just like most people, she was just unfortunate to have an overly active conscience.

"Oh, he is. He was up at the crack of dawn this morning. I don't know how he does it."

Jane failed to come up with an interesting follow-up question that would convey interest and concern, muttering instead something about the health service and consultants being overworked. Sara, seeming impatient with her friend's trite observation, ran her hands gently over Senan's mop of golden hair, choosing not to respond.

Knowing that she couldn't launch straight into questions about John Davy, Jane took her cue from the mother's adoring gesture and admired the younger boy's hair. He stared at her boldly, amused and terrified in equal measure. She felt that most babies reacted to her this way and that it was probably due to her hair colour and complexion. He seemed to find in her an interesting subject worthy of his undivided attention. There was an openness to him that was not apparent in the older child, perhaps due more to age than character. Eoin had a supercilious expression, not unlike that of his father.

Sara's eyes flitted randomly from one diner to the next, a habit which Jane suddenly remembered from their college days. Although Sara followed their conversation diligently, never missing a detail, filing every name away for future reference, her watchfulness had a discomfiting effect on Jane, who could not help but feel that as a subject she was not enough for Sara's roaming mind.

Much to Jane's relief, Sara abhorred small talk. They both agreed that there was nothing more draining than resharing the same content with multiple, equally bored listeners. Their active minds longed for new information to parse and analyse. Remembering this, Jane abandoned the question she was formulating in her mind about feeder schools and Irish language immersion.

Gordon, despite his fiercely Protestant name, was the son of a native Irish speaker from the West of Ireland who spoke only his mother tongue at home with his children. Irish language education had become increasingly popular with the middle classes in recent decades. Whether or not Gordon spoke Irish at home with his children was not an entirely uninteresting subject, but not necessarily an avenue she wanted to go down that day.

"So," Jane intertwined her fingers and rested her chin on her knuckles, in an effort to appear more relaxed.

She resolved to ask the question she may not want to hear answered. She had to do it. She reassured herself that half the world was getting a divorce or was already divorced or wishing they were divorced. "Did you manage to find anything more on John?"

Sara hesitated, perhaps bewildered by Jane's directness, and appeared to gather her thoughts before replying frankly, "Oh God, well, if it was only one thing it wouldn't be so bad. I really could not believe he was capable of it."

As love's promise crumbled before her, Jane's heart sank with a weight that only the gravest disappointment could bestow. All composure abandoned her as she buried her head in her hands, "What is it? What has he done?"

Jane peered through her parted fingers at Sara, whose delivery and cadence would have been more suited to a news report from a warzone than an open and frank conversation between two old college friends. "He had a six-year affair with Dee O'Callaghan."

"What? Are you sure? That makes no sense. They broke up, and she married his friend and had kids with him. Why wouldn't he just have stayed with Dee, if that's what he wanted?"

Her breath caught, and she suddenly felt adrift in a sea of uncertainty. She grasped the table, in an attempt to anchor herself in this new reality, far worse than her imagination could ever have tormented her with.

"Why? Because he's a shit, and so is Dee. The rules don't apply to them." Sara sighed wearily. "They had hooked up once, said it was a mistake, swore to themselves and each other that it would never happen again. But it did."

"So, this was a full-blown affair?" Jane grappled to find some justification for his behaviour. "Were he and Liz still together at the time? Is it possible they had separated but were still living together?"

Sara scoffed. "The affair started just after he and Liz got married. She has three kids, you know. One or two of them must have been conceived during the affair."

"That can't be right!" Jane's first instinct was to grab her phone from her handbag. She would have to clear this up immediately. It was one thing to have an affair, but this bordered on leading a double life. She placed her phone back on the table. She stood a better chance of getting the full picture here and now from Sara. She inhaled deeply and exhaled with such vigour that both Eoin and an elderly woman at a nearby table turned to stare at her. "But why didn't they just leave their partners? Couples reunite all the time; it wouldn't have been that strange if they got back together. I mean, John and Dee were a couple for, what— two, three years in college?"

"Oh, you're assuming it was an affair of the heart. It was probably just sex. Knowing them."

Sara seemed to be very well acquainted with both John and Dee's inner workings. As painful as this revelation was for Jane, she needed to find out as much as she could while she had Sara in front of her. She hated nothing more than being in the dark. Forewarned, forearmed – wasn't that what her mother had always said?

"How did Liz find out?"

"Caroline was a bit sketchy on the details. She was under the impression that John owned up, but I think it's more likely he got caught out."

"And that took six years? He must be a master of deception. I mean, I can't believe he would be capable of such deceit."

"Dee's husband is very naïve. It wouldn't surprise me if she sleeps around with men from all over the place. She's the female version of John."

"And this is all filtered through John? It's his version of events?" Jane dreaded to think what the unfiltered version was like.

"Yes, entirely, but Caroline seemed to think that John had held up his hands and taken full responsibility at the time. Disgusted by his past actions, a different man today, blah, blah, blah."

"Is that even possible? I mean, six years, that's a sustained lie. And there was no need for the secrecy. They could have left their partners and been honest. People would not have been that shocked." Jane couldn't wrap her head around how unnecessary the subterfuge had been. "And where do they stand now?"

Jane contemplated how desperate she would appear if she were to accept the crumbs that John now had to offer. Was there any way they could continue as a couple without her looking like a desperate fool? Did she even want to?

"It's all over. Dee said she couldn't do it to her husband, she couldn't leave her kids, so despite promises of making a new life together she pulled out at the last minute, and he was apparently heartbroken."

"Then it *was* an affair of the heart! It wasn't purely about sex, if they had planned to build a future together."

"Oh, Jane, who knows? All this regret on his part – I got the feeling that Caroline didn't buy it. I mean, they're friends, but she's a straight talker. And she said he was almost enjoying the shock value of it all. That he was, I don't know, wallowing and somehow excusing his behaviour because Dee was the love of his life. But she wasn't the only one. He wasn't long getting back in the dating game. He slept with his neighbour, and that turned out to be a bit of a mess, because she was engaged at the time."

"I knew it! We passed her on the stairs, and she totally blanked him. He was acting all nonchalant, but she's too beautiful for him not to notice. I should have listened to my instincts."

"Listen, Jane, there's more—" Sara paused as the waitress came to take their order.

Jane could hardly think of food at a time like this. As soon as Sara had ordered for herself and the children, Jane requested the chowder, already knowing she wouldn't eat a bite.

"Oh God." Feeling her eyes start to well up, Jane willed herself not to cry, as Eoin gave her for the first time his undivided attention.

Sara ploughed on. "Some young woman is pregnant by him. She's a student teacher, a primary teacher, not exactly in Tilly's school, but there's some connection there. They met on Tinder."

"What is he doing visiting me and making plans to introduce me to his parents next weekend if he's having a child with another woman?" Jane searched Sara's face for some sign that she might have the answer, but she stared back blankly. "Why did he drag me into this mess? He went out of his way to track me down, and I thought it was because there had always been something special between us, but now—" Jane's voice trailed off.

"Be grateful that you've found out now, instead of six months down the line, after you've introduced him to your family and friends. Or worse, after you've gotten engaged."

"So, is he actually in a relationship with the mother of his baby? Oh, I don't even care. Oh, but I do."

"I don't think they even speak, really."

"And he's admitted to getting this young woman pregnant, to his friends, his family?"

"He actually went to Liz with the news first, to tip her off that some young woman was claiming to be pregnant with his child."

"Oh, so he didn't even remember her?"

"Well, it shows how many one night stands he's had. It's very much like something you'd expect from an NBA star or a member of a now-defunct rock group."

"When was he going to tell me? If Caroline knows, does he not think it would filter back to me eventually?"

"You'd think so, wouldn't you?" Sara turned her attention to Senan, who had started to regurgitate his milk from earlier.

Jane felt an unexpected tenderness towards the young boy. It was time for her, she supposed, to re-imagine a new future, one without John Davy in it.

CHAPTER TWENTY-NINE
Aftermath

All the while she had marvelled at the stupidity of Cathy Killeen's husband, cuckolded in plain sight, she herself had been the victim of John Davy's deception. He had paraded her around his daughter's birthday party, where everyone except her had known about his antics. No wonder they had looked at her with a mixture of pity and disdain. The thought of John, with his receding hairline and thickening waist, seducing a young teacher sickened her to the pit of her stomach.

With Sara's help, she had found the girl online. Her profile picture showed her and another girl also in her early twenties sticking out their tongues at the camera. She had a pretty face that was plump and inoffensive but was definitely not his usual type. No matter how long or from which angle she stared at this young woman, she could not decide if she were more or less attractive than her. But what did it matter, anyway, if she had been a supermodel or a hobbit?

John's behaviour was despicable, and the whole affair was unsavoury. What on earth had he been thinking pursuing Jane at all when he had so many skeletons in his closet? It was clear to her in that moment that he had never had any long-term intentions in her regard. To him, she had only ever been something to pass the time, to distract from the embarrassing mess he had made of his life, to create a veneer of respectability where none existed. Confronting him now would expose her vulnerability, it would lay bare the emotional investment she had already made. He would surely laugh at her naivety, her downright stupidity in thinking this was ever going to be any more than a casual, half-hearted sort of affair, which was doubtless running concurrently with many others.

When it was approaching midnight, despite promising herself she would not call him until at least the next morning, she dialled his personal mobile. It went straight to voicemail, and she felt a wave of relief wash over her. She considered for one wild moment sending a text message to convey her anger, but she quickly concluded that she was worth more than that. Casual friendships, tennis coaching, book club attendance: they were all things that could be ended with a text message or an unreturned call. But she had invested her entire soul in this relationship.

Much as she longed to conceal from him the degree of hurt and betrayal she felt, she knew the only way she would achieve full and proper closure was to confront him. She consulted the address book in her phone to find his work mobile number. She had never called it until now. She was surprised that he would even have given it to her in the first place. He would not have her number saved in this phone, which would make him either more or less likely to pick up.

Three rings later, he answered. It was as if she were standing across from him. With the dull ache in her chest slowly building, she sat down on her bed. The seconds of awkward silence bloated into almost half a minute. He knew. It was why he dared not ask her what was wrong. He waited for her to find the words.

"John, you've left a lot out."

"Yes," he replied calmly, sounding almost relieved that the moment had caught up with him. "I had to. I guess you know about everything."

"Not everything, I'm sure. I'm certain there are lots of things you'll barely admit to yourself, never mind me, but yeah, I know about the affair with Dee and the young woman."

"Well, there's no point me denying any of it. I made mistakes."

Jane scoffed at his choice of words. "I think they were more than just mistakes."

She waited for him to break into a stream of apologies before begging her to forgive him, to help him be a better person, to stick with him, even though he didn't deserve it. Nothing. No wonder the sex had been so infrequent and lacklustre. They had never been exclusive, and he'd had no notion of staying faithful to her. That part of it all made sense now. But nothing else did.

"I guess that's it, then." His tone was resigned. She detected a hint of relief in it.

Had his goal all along been to drive her away? To drive all the women away? She wanted to hate him in that moment. She had every right to rage furiously against the man who'd wasted so much of her time. But for all her self-righteousness, she could not summon a spark of anger.

How could she not have seen it all along? He would never have enough. He would always search for more, for different, for new. This knowledge hovered in the silent ether between them. It was even more powerful for being unspoken. He ended the call, and she sank back on her bed.

CHAPTER THIRTY
The Guest List

Corrections were endless. Summer exams were always the worst. Jane's mother arrived in her old childhood bedroom far too regularly with home-baked scones and milky tea. Jane didn't have the heart to remind Claire that she was avoiding all sugar in the run-up to Margaret's wedding. In recent weeks, her life had spiralled so quickly out of control that she felt her weight was the one thing she could determine.

Jane couldn't identify what or how she was feeling since her split from John. She wouldn't describe it as heartache – it didn't deserve that label. She had not shed one single tear since he confirmed that he was, in fact, a cheat and a liar. She was experiencing a mixture of anger, at herself, for wasting her entire adulthood pining after John Davy; and shock, that the man she had idealised had revealed himself to be a complete mess. He hadn't begged for her forgiveness or tried to explain the unexplainable. He had, like a turtle, pulled his neck back inside his shell and pottered off. It had meant nothing to him.

Frank had phoned Jane early that May, to ensure that Margaret was allowing her to help. His fiercely independent fiancée liked nothing more than organising, and nothing less than importuning others. But Jane had reassured him that Margaret had been very good at delegating tasks to her closest friends. Jane had been assigned the job of designing the invitations and sending them to the guest list, which comprised forty family members and close friends.

It was to be a very small ceremony, followed by a meal in Buswell's Hotel on Molesworth Street. For Jane, it had an old-world charm seldom found in flashy city centre hotels these days. She could imagine it as the setting for an Agatha Christie murder mystery.

For the invitation cards, Jane had drawn a little cartoon, in which she'd effortlessly captured Margaret's mischievous sense of humour in her impish grin. They were posted, at very short notice, to people who were close enough to Margaret and Frank to cancel any other plans they might have had to be there for this special day.

The second time Frank called her was to thank her for the beautiful illustration of him and Margaret. She had felt considerably less pleased with her portrayal of Frank. Having rarely seen him smile, turning up the corners of his mouth and adding laughter lines around his eyes felt like a betrayal of sorts. He was one of life's serious people, and that was perfectly acceptable, she saw that now. What did it matter what she thought of his dry disposition? All that mattered was how Margaret felt about him. Frank had also asked for one of the invitations to be redone. William was no longer with that English girl, Natalie. He felt it might be less awkward to address it to only William. He would, after all, be sitting at the singles table, as Jane herself would be.

Jane had happily obliged.

CHAPTER THIRTY-ONE
Anniversary

Charlotte and Neil arrived together on the Sunday morning of the bank holiday weekend. Her mother fussed over them as Jane lingered in her bedroom. Charlotte had brought anniversary gifts for their parents, who were forty years married that weekend. Jane abhorred the performative element of it all, the way her mother repeatedly thanked her younger daughter for a scarf she would never wear. Their father would be equally eager to ensure Charlotte was happy, nodding his enthusiastic approval at whatever tie she'd selected and smiling wryly at the funny reference in the card.

Happy Charlotte, happy house, he had so often said over the years. Some people were just easier to love, and that certainly was the case when it came to Charlotte, as far as their parents were concerned, and as far as Jane could see. She never doubted their devotion to and interest in her sister. That had translated to all other areas of her life, Charlotte never questioned her likeability, her attractiveness, her sex appeal. And people responded to that. Her poor simple parents, good people, had never understood their elder, aloof daughter. She could finally see why. She would struggle to like herself with her haughty disposition, always watchful and judgemental.

The only saving grace about her relationship with John was that she had kept it a secret from her family and work colleagues, except for Margaret, of course. There was nothing more humiliating than being quizzed on a recently disintegrated relationship around a school staffroom table. The young female teachers in St Mary's were painfully predictable, engaged and married by their late twenties, pregnant within two years, and always on the lookout for the glimmer of a diamond on the ring finger of the eligible female staff members.

She entered the sitting room with her head bowed and shoulders rounded, wanting in equal measure to avoid a hug from Neil and to be the type of person to whom demonstrations of affection came easily. But if she were going to start doling out hugs nilly-willy, she'd rather not start with Neil. Luckily, he avoided meeting her gaze until she acknowledged him from the safety of her favourite armchair, far removed from the sofa where he lounged with Charlotte, who was heavily pregnant.

"Oh Jane, you're going to love your present." Charlotte signalled to Neil to get the present from the bag at his feet.

"What did you get me a present for?"

"Your birthday! I missed it, remember?"

"I'll save it till later, after dinner, maybe. I like to have something to look forward to."

Charlotte crinkled her nose in excitement. Jane tried to remember if she had texted Charlotte on her birthday in March. Their father, Séamus, shuffled in wearing his new Ugg slippers. They had been his most recent Christmas gift from Charlotte. He laid his hand firmly on Neil's shoulder in acknowledgement of his arrival, not feeling the need for hugs or handshakes.

"Aren't you going to a wedding soon, Jane?" Neil enquired. "Weddings are great for single people. You never know who you might meet."

He squeezed Charlotte's hand to indicate that they had met at a wedding, as if Jane needed to be reminded. Fighting the urge to bristle at the inference that she needed to be part of a couple to be happy, Jane smiled a seraphic smile. A hopefulness hovered at the edges of her consciousness. She was slow to grasp for it; in case she scared it away.

She was, indeed, looking forward to Margaret's wedding. The melancholy that had been her bedfellow for the last few months seemed to have lifted. William suddenly sprung to mind and she wondered what he might be doing on this bright Sunday morning, and if it were possible that he had something to do with this new and unexpected lightness of heart.

Printed in Dunstable, United Kingdom